Suzanne Lissaman is a British romantic comedy writer who lives in the middle of England with her husband, children, and a demanding but adorable cat. She's also an artist and photographer.

The first novel in the Dashford series, *Be More Octopus,* won the Romantic Novelists' Association Debut Romantic Novel Award 2024.

Be one of the first people to hear about Suzanne's latest books and freebies by signing up for her book club. You'll find the link on her website:

https://www.suzannelissaman.com

You might find the occasional cat picture, too.

ALSO BY SUZANNE LISSAMAN

The Dashford Comedies

Be More Octopus (Book 1)
Be More Lucy (Book 2)

BE LESS PANDA

The Dashford Comedies Book 3

Suzanne Lissaman

An Octosulis Publishing paperback

First published in Great Britain in 2024

ISBN-13: 978-1-7393575-3-5

For R, D and Z

love you all xxx

Part One

February 2020

1

Ping. Not another text! Em was finding it hard enough to concentrate on her job this morning without more interruptions. She looked at her phone. It was a message from her husband, Jack.

```
Have you told Nancy yet?
```

Em tapped out her reply:

```
No. She's still not back.
```

She sent a second text, hoping it would stop him asking her again:

```
She often stays for a drink at the
Fisherman's Arms after her wild swimming
session.
```

Three dots appeared.

```
Ok - let me know when she knows xx
```

Em sighed.

```
I will - I haven't forgotten that's what
we agreed
```

That could come across as a bit terse, her inner voice warned her. She added a smiley emoji and a couple of Xs before pressing the send arrow.

Em pushed her chair back to get nearer to the warmth of the Aga - one of the benefits of working in Dashford Grange's kitchen on a cold winter's day. She ought to get back to updating the holiday cottage booking spreadsheet but she'd allow herself one more look at the photo first. She bent down to her bag and pulled out the small folder containing the flimsy piece of paper. She smiled at the fuzzy black-and-white image. *You're going to wear it out at this rate.* She photographed it with her phone so she'd be able to look at it on there in future. The original could go in an album when she got home this afternoon.

It was funny how this little piece of paper finally made it seem real. Ever since that blue line had appeared on the pregnancy test, it had felt like a dream. Now, with a bit of luck, she was going to be a mother by the end of the summer.

'Hello!' Her boss, Nancy, walked into the kitchen. 'And how are you this morning?'

'I'm fine, thanks.'

'You seem on edge. Anything you want to tell me?'

Em swore Nancy was psychic. 'Yes, I have, actually. Jack and I - we're, umm ...'

She'd rehearsed this so many times. Why was it so difficult to say it out loud? 'We're going to be parents.'

Nancy grinned. 'End of August, by any chance?'

Em laughed. 'My due date is 24th August. How did you know?'

'You've been looking peaky since Christmas, and you hardly drank anything at your wedding. Olivia's thrilled.'

Olivia was Jack's mother and also Nancy's oldest and closest friend.

'But we haven't told Olivia yet.'

If Jack had said anything to Olivia before the 13-week scan, she'd have told everyone "in the strictest confidence" and Em didn't want anyone to know until her pregnancy stood a reasonable chance of going full-term.

'I'm sure she'll pretend to be surprised when Jack breaks the news. When is he telling her?' Nancy asked.

'When I text him to say I've told you,' Em said, picking up her phone.

'I'll make us some tea to celebrate.'

Em smiled. Nancy's answer to everything was a cup of Earl Grey. Em tapped out a message to Jack.

```
Your mum already knows - Nancy guessed
weeks ago! xx
```

His reply was almost instant:

```
Really?? Xx
```

Em texted her best friend Lucy next. Lucy already knew, but Em had sworn her to secrecy, even making her promise not to tell her partner, Mark.

```
All fine. You can tell Mark now.
```

Lucy replied with a thumbs-up emoji.

Em went back to her work. A few minutes later, Lucy texted her back.

```
He knew! Jack told him weeks ago.
```

This was ridiculous. 'Has somebody taken an announcement out in The Times?' Em said to Nancy. 'I was looking forward to surprising everyone, but you've all worked it out already!'

'You don't normally phone me on a Thursday morning.'

'I wanted you to be one of the first to hear my news.' *Or, at this rate, the last.* Em heard him shout, 'Cynthia! Come here, darling. Em's on the phone.'

Em was so eager to tell him that she didn't wait for her soon-to-be stepmother to arrive. 'You're going to a grandad in the summer.'

'That's me £10 down then,' he laughed.

'That wasn't what I was expecting you to say!' Was no one going to be surprised? None of the pregnancy sites she'd been avidly reading had said anything about family and friends being this laid back about your big announcement.

'Sorry, love. It's just that at your wedding Cynthia bet me that you were already pregnant. I thought if I'd not heard anything by the end of this month, I'd be in the clear.'

Olivia was Jack's mother and also Nancy's oldest and closest friend.

'But we haven't told Olivia yet.'

If Jack had said anything to Olivia before the 13-week scan, she'd have told everyone "in the strictest confidence" and Em didn't want anyone to know until her pregnancy stood a reasonable chance of going full-term.

'I'm sure she'll pretend to be surprised when Jack breaks the news. When is he telling her?' Nancy asked.

'When I text him to say I've told you,' Em said, picking up her phone.

'I'll make us some tea to celebrate.'

Em smiled. Nancy's answer to everything was a cup of Earl Grey. Em tapped out a message to Jack.

```
Your mum already knows - Nancy guessed
weeks ago! xx
```

His reply was almost instant:

```
Really?? Xx
```

Em texted her best friend Lucy next. Lucy already knew, but Em had sworn her to secrecy, even making her promise not to tell her partner, Mark.

```
All fine. You can tell Mark now.
```

Lucy replied with a thumbs-up emoji.

Em went back to her work. A few minutes later, Lucy texted her back.

```
He knew! Jack told him weeks ago.
```

This was ridiculous. 'Has somebody taken an announcement out in The Times?' Em said to Nancy. 'I was looking forward to surprising everyone, but you've all worked it out already!'

Nancy tried to reassure her. 'I'm sure there are some people who don't know.'

'A few monks in Outer Mongolia might have missed the news, I suppose.'

'It's fairly obvious to anyone who knows you well.'

Em smiled. 'I guess it doesn't matter now. The important thing is the baby is well.'

'Have you got a scan picture?' Nancy asked as she put a steaming mug of tea down on Em's desk.

Em showed her the photo on her phone.

'Amazing, isn't it, seeing them before they're even born. I didn't have that with my first.' Nancy zoomed in on the image. 'I think it's a boy. And he's definitely got Jack's nose.'

'Really?' Em didn't want to refer to the baby as he or she yet, though Jack had named them Bob. "Just as a temporary name. We can't keep referring to our first child as it," he'd insisted.

Em looked at the scan picture again. The baby's head hadn't got much of a nose at all yet, though if Bob did end up with Jack's nose, that wouldn't be a bad thing. Jack's was fairly appealing as noses went.

'Is your father pleased?' Nancy asked.

'Hopefully, he will be. I haven't told him yet because his fiancée is as bad at keeping secrets as Olivia is.'

'Why don't you tell him now? I've got some washing to put away. I'll leave you to it.'

'Before you go, this came for you.' Em handed Nancy an envelope that had arrived in this morning's post. It had a German stamp, and the address was handwritten. Em guessed it might be from the friend Nancy had visited in Berlin last year.

Nancy gasped. An unusual reaction for a personal letter. 'Is everything ok?' Em asked.

'Yes, yes. It's just … I'll take my tea in my study.' Nancy said, dashing out of the kitchen just as Jack phoned.

'How is my gorgeous wife?' he asked.

'I don't know about the gorgeous one, but the tired and queasy one is fine. I'm not sure Nancy is, though. I've never seen her so flustered.'

'She'll be wondering what to do about your maternity leave.'

'No, it's not that. She was fine until I gave her a letter. She went very pale, and she's not even opened it yet.'

'I guess she'll tell you soon enough.' Jack didn't sound that bothered. 'But if you're interested, I have told Bob's future grandmother.'

Oh yes, Olivia. How could Em have forgotten? Baby brain must've kicked in already. 'Sorry! I should've asked. How did it go?'

'She did a fabulous job of pretending she didn't know that she was getting a new grandchild. She sends her love.'

Time to challenge him about blabbing to his best friend. 'I gather you've already told Mark?'

'Ah, yes.' He sounded sheepish. 'It accidentally slipped out.'

At least he was being honest. 'When?'

'Um … The day you did the pregnancy test.' Jack sounded even more uncomfortable now.

'That long ago? Why didn't you say?'

'I thought you'd be upset.'

He was right. Very upset. But there was no point in berating him now. 'At least it's not a secret anymore.'

'Have you told your dad yet?'

'No. But I'm just about to. See you later.'

Em dialled her father's number.

He answered straightaway. 'Hello, love. Is everything ok?'

'Yes. Why do you ask?'

'You don't normally phone me on a Thursday morning.'

'I wanted you to be one of the first to hear my news.' *Or, at this rate, the last.* Em heard him shout, 'Cynthia! Come here, darling. Em's on the phone.'

Em was so eager to tell him that she didn't wait for her soon-to-be stepmother to arrive. 'You're going to a grandad in the summer.'

'That's me £10 down then,' he laughed.

'That wasn't what I was expecting you to say!' Was no one going to be surprised? None of the pregnancy sites she'd been avidly reading had said anything about family and friends being this laid back about your big announcement.

'Sorry, love. It's just that at your wedding Cynthia bet me that you were already pregnant. I thought if I'd not heard anything by the end of this month, I'd be in the clear.'

2

Lucy put down her phone and leaned back in her office chair just as her PA, Kizzy, walked in.

'You look miles away,' Kizzy said.

'I was thinking about how everything's going to change now.'

'Why? I've warned you not to make any big decisions while Mercury is in retrograde.'

'I fail to see how the position of the planets affects the lives of me and my friends,' Lucy said, immediately regretting it when she spotted Kizzy picking up a marker pen from the tray on the whiteboard. 'I don't need diagrams,' she added.

'You clearly do because I've been through this with you before.'

'And I didn't believe it last time either.'

'It's up to you, but if you make serious decisions between now and the 9th March, you'll regret it. My Auntie Beryl ignored that advice, and look what happened to her.'

Kizzy always had a relative with a story to illustrate whatever point she was trying to make, but she was part of such a large family it was difficult to keep track of who was who.

'Is she the one who married the bigamist?' Lucy asked.

'No. That's her sister. Auntie Beryl bought a car while Mercury was in retrograde, and it ended up in the river with her in it.'

'Are you saying Mercury's gravitational pull caused it to veer off the road?'

'Don't be ridiculous. She mistook the accelerator for the brake pedal and went careering across the car park and over the bank into the water. She was alright, but the car was a write-off.'

'I see. Well, thank you for your sage advice, but ...'

'You're going to ignore it again, aren't you?' Kizzy folded her arms and gave Lucy one of her disapproving looks.

'I was going to say I have no control over this particular major change. Em is pregnant.'

Kizzy's demeanour changed completely. 'That's wonderful news! You're going to be a ... ' she looked puzzled. 'What are you going to be?'

It was a fair question. 'I guess I'll be one of those aunties who's not actually an auntie and annoys Jack and Em by turning up with lots of bad stuff to spoil their child.'

Lucy was looking forward to that, but the downside was the new arrival was bound to change her relationship with her best friend for the first few years, at least. Once Carver Junior arrived, Em wouldn't have time to jump on a call to discuss Lucy's latest dilemma, and Lucy wasn't in a position to help Em with child-rearing advice. Lucy had seen it already with their mutual friend Ella. Everything revolved around the baby, and she hadn't even given birth yet.

'Will they ask you to be a godmother?' Kizzy asked.

'I think that would be a bit hypocritical, don't you? Neither Em nor I have set foot in a church except for the occasional wedding or funeral. Though I'm not sure where Jack stands on all that.'

Was Jack religious? Em had never mentioned it, and they'd married in a registry office, so it was unlikely. Though being divorced, Jack wouldn't have been allowed to marry in church. But weren't they more lenient about that now? She'd have to ask Mark when she got home later. As his best friend since childhood, Mark would know - unless Jack had discovered religion during that couple of years when they'd fallen out with one another.

'Lucy!'

'Sorry, I was just pondering Jack's religious beliefs.'

Kizzy huffed. 'I hope you don't think I'm speaking out of turn, but you keep disappearing off in a daydream lately.'

'Do I?'

'Yes. You did it yesterday in that meeting with Harry. She was trying to engage you in what strategy you thought best for marketing those hideous toilet seats, and you kept gazing out of the window. I hope she doesn't get fed up and clear off to another company.'

Lucy hoped that, too. Having her business partner stay in the office here in Birmingham was key to Lucy and Mark's big plan to go globetrotting later this year. Harry would be looking after face-to-face client meetings while Lucy did all the creative strategy stuff remotely, in between visiting scenic locations and downing the occasional margarita by the pool. Meanwhile, Mark would be doing whatever he was going to do, which was up for debate now that he'd walked out on his temporary solicitor's job after less than a week.

'I can't stand being stuck in the office,' he'd said. 'My mind keeps straying back to sun, sea and sand, and there isn't much of any of those in Birmingham in February, apart from the big pile of sand on the building site next door.'

Lucy hadn't been surprised. Swapping running his own jet ski hire business on the Costa del Sol for going back to poring over property contracts was never going to be easy.

'Lucy! You're doing it again. Are you sure you're getting enough sleep?'

Perhaps that was the problem. She hadn't had much rest since Mark moved in last month. They had a lot of lost time to make up for.

'I think my nocturnal activities are my business. Now, are you going to get me that latte I asked for?'

Kizzy pointed to the takeout coffee cup and raised her eyebrows.

Shit. Had she really missed Kizzy putting it down next to her? She was going to have to try to get more sleep. Or a holiday. Now, that was an interesting thought. With Mark no longer tied down by a job, there was nothing to stop them from starting their travel plans sooner.

'I've got a little project for you this afternoon, Kizz. Go through my diary between now and the end of March, and work out which week I can easily work remotely. Then sort out some flights to Venice for me and Mark.'

'That comes under the category of "big decision",' a disapproving Kizzy replied.

'Technically, it's not. I'm bringing an existing decision forward, that's all. Mark and I agreed at Christmas that we'd start with a test trip to Italy. I've no idea what Mercury was up to them, but I'm pretty sure it wasn't retrograde.'

Kizzy grudgingly picked up her notepad. 'Return flights?'

Lucy shook her head. 'We can stop with my folks in Tuscany after a couple of days in Venice, then fly back from Florence. Find somewhere swanky to stay in Venice with good wifi. I need to confirm that working remotely is really possible.'

3

Nancy closed the door to her study and sat down in her chair. She put the letter on the desk in front of her and took a deep breath to steady herself. She hadn't seen that neat handwriting for over 50 years, and she'd never expected to see it again.

She picked up the letter again and sniffed it. It smelled of paper. *Did you expect it to smell of him, you old fool? No point looking at it, Nancy Smith. Open it!*

Smith. Funny how her inner voice admonished her using her maiden name. She'd been a Farnham for how long? 49 years. She and Xander would be celebrating their golden wedding anniversary next year if he hadn't had that stupid heart attack. Not that it was much of a marriage. He'd probably been faithful to her for a year at most. But she knew all about his flirtatious ways with women before she married him. After all, he'd used his charms to get her into bed with him as well. She should never have marched into that register office and said, 'I will'. But then, if she hadn't, she wouldn't have Nigel and Mark. And after all that funny business in Paris, at least becoming Mrs Farnham had given her an air of respectability.

Stop procrastinating! She put the envelope back on the desk while she searched in the top drawer for her father's old letter opener. If this letter was from the person she suspected it was from, it deserved to be opened neatly. At the back of the drawer behind a large roll of parcel tape, she found the miniature silver sword with Joan of Arc clasping the handle at the top. Her father had probably used it all those years ago to open the letter she sent him saying she wouldn't be coming back to Coventry.

She carefully inserted the tip of the blade into the small gap at the top corner of the envelope, slowly eased it under the flap, and then angled it away from herself, quickly pushing it away from the envelope. It made a satisfying tearing sound as it cut through the first half of the flap. She repeated the movement to complete the job. She gulped. It was open now.

She took another deep breath before slipping her fingers inside the envelope to pull out its contents - a matching single sheet of good-quality paper. It was filled with writing in the same hand as the address. She unfolded it and began to read.

Part Two

1964

4

'Happy New Year!' Olivia shouted in Nancy's ear as the crowds jostled around them.

'Happy New Year!' Nancy shouted back just as she was shoved in the back by a drunken man trying to make his way to Nelson's column. 'Whose idea was this again?' she laughed.

'It's better than being stuck at home with my parents. I should have stayed in Paris. I bet the celebrations are a lot more civilised there,' Olivia replied as they watched another drunken reveller attempt to climb the Trafalgar Square Christmas Tree.

A man clutching a beer bottle staggered up to Nancy. 'Happy Christmas, darlin'!'

'I think you're a week late for that.' Nancy said, rolling her eyes.

'Stuck up cow,' he growled and walked off, managing to spill some of his beer down Nancy's new coat as he went.

'Not the best start to 1964.' Olivia handed Nancy a handkerchief.

'No,' Nancy said thoughtfully as she dabbed at the damp patch left by the beer. 'Let's hope it improves.'

'We may as well head back home before things turn nasty.' Olivia grabbed Nancy's hand, and they weaved their way through the crowds and onto Pall Mall. 'The tube's going to be a nightmare. Let's walk.'

They headed in the general direction of Chelsea, where Olivia's parents owned a large townhouse with views over the River Thames.

'So what's your New Year's resolution?' Olivia asked as soon as the crowds had thinned enough for them to walk side by side.

'To save enough money to join Patty's yacht crew.'

'Has she still got that mad idea of sailing around the world?'

Ever since Olivia and Nancy had first met Patty at school, she'd been hatching plans for ambitious sailing trips.

Nancy was annoyed. 'It's not mad at all. Men have been doing it for centuries.'

'In large sailing ships, not little yachts.'

'Patty's bought a big ocean-going yacht, nothing like the little things you've watched me manoeuvre around Dashford Bay.'

'I don't care how big it is, the only way you're getting me on a yacht is if it involves a champagne reception with canapés.'

'I'm sure we'll get champagne at the end,' Nancy laughed.

'After months at sea! You'll be positively feral by the time you get back to Portsmouth.'

'We get a few stops en route. It will be a big improvement on spending the winter sitting in an office. You've got no sense of adventure!'

'How does that fit in with being groomed to take over the family business?'

'You really think my father wants me to take over running his beloved factory? He thinks all women are fit for is keeping a nice home and producing babies. I'm allowed to do some secretarial work to keep me out of mischief until a suitable man is willing to marry me, but that's all. Not that running a factory is my idea of fun.'

'Manufacturing car headlights not lighting you up, then?' Olivia grinned.

'Ha ha!' Nancy had no desire to spend the rest of her life working at G Smith and Son Ltd. She was only tolerating it now to save enough money to fund her place on Patty's trip. Her grandfather had set up the business in a small garage in the centre of Coventry in the 1920s, but now her father ran the large sprawling factory it had evolved into. When he retired, there would only be Nancy and her older brother Eddie in line to take control. And Eddie was a budding actor who preferred much more artistic pursuits.

'Has he given up on Eddie ever taking an interest in manufacturing?' Olivia asked.

'I think so. Eddie's got his sights set on Hollywood. And I don't mean the one in Birmingham. Car headlights are nowhere near as appealing as film set lights as far as Eddie is concerned. What about you?'

'I can't say that I've considered car part manufacturing as a career.'

Nancy chuckled. 'I meant your New Year's resolution.'

'I'm not bothering with one of those this year. I'm enjoying life in France. I don't want that to change for a while.' Olivia looked thoughtful. 'If you're fed up, why don't you come and live with me?'

'I'd need a visa or something. And what would I do?'

'Paint views of the Seine?'

'You remember what our art teacher used to say to me? "Even Jackson Pollock would consider your creations messy, Nancy."'

'Write a book, then. You were much better than me in English Language classes.'

'And how will that earn me enough money by June?'

'June? I thought Patty was planning to set sail in September?'

'She is, but she needs my financial contribution by June, and even if it was September, I'd have barely finished the first draft of a book by then, let alone got a publishing deal. Looks like I'm stuck in Coventry for the time being.'

'It's not like you to be this negative.'

'I'm sorry. The postman delivered a Christmas card from Billy before I left home yesterday.'

'The Hot Ozzie?' Olivia grinned. She obviously remembered Nancy's racy tales of how she'd spent last summer on the North Devon coast. 'And what did he have to say for himself?'

'He won't be able to get over here from Australia again. He's getting married.' Nancy tried to hide her disappointment, but Olivia knew her too well.

'You were expecting him to come back, weren't you?'

'I suppose I hoped he would.' Nancy sighed. Billy, with his cheeky attitude and, let's face it, very fit body, had been the most exciting thing that had happened to her so far. He'd taught her how to surf and a lot more than besides. English men, at least the ones in her social circle, were plain dull by comparison.

'You didn't fall in love with him, did you?'

'No.' Nancy wasn't so sure about that. 'He was just fun, that's all. I feel like I'm stuck in a rut.'

'So join me in Paris. There are plenty of attractive, eligible men there.'

'I'm not looking for love. There's no point if I'm only going to be there for a few months. I don't need a man holding me back.'

'We'll see,' Olivia said, not looking convinced. 'As you need to earn a living, you could work in the English bookshop near my apartment. They're always looking for new staff. Father dearest knows the owner, Madame Dubois. She seems charming whenever I go in there. I'm sure he could pull a few strings to get your paperwork sorted quickly.'

Olivia's father was a civil servant who did something important in the Foreign Office, which probably explained how Olivia had got a job as a translator at NATO HQ as soon as she'd graduated from Oxford last year.

'I don't think my French is good enough. It wasn't my favourite subject at school. I wouldn't have got any marks at all if I hadn't copied your homework,' Nancy said.

Olivia had always been top of the class. Her regular summer holidays to the Dordogne must have helped. But as there wasn't much call for speaking French in Devon or Coventry, Nancy doubted she could even manage to introduce herself now.

'You don't need to be fluent. You'll be dealing with customers who can read English. And you'll be amazed how much you'll pick up just by being surrounded by French people.'

Nancy and Olivia walked on in silence for a few minutes while Nancy pondered Olivia's suggestion. It would beat being wolf-whistled at by the men in the press shop whenever she had to walk the length of the factory. And the bookshop job would probably pay as much as her current one, given how little her father thought she was worth. But there was a flaw in the plan.

'I can't see my loving, caring papa going for that suggestion,' she said. 'Education is wasted on girls, Nancy,' she added, doing a passable impression of her father in rant mode. He'd quashed any hopes she'd had of going to university, so she very much doubted he'd be up for funding a trip abroad, particularly Paris. His opinion of the French was unrepeatable for reasons he wasn't prepared to divulge, but he implied it had something to do with the war.

'Why don't you tell him that improving your foreign language skills would help the factory's export department?' Olivia suggested.

'But I don't want to work in the export department. I can't think of anything worse. They're not exactly the most dynamic of people. Audrey never smiles and reeks of mothballs. And her manager, Alec, has raging halitosis and no idea that deodorant has been invented, which is rather unfortunate given he only ever wears nylon shirts.'

'But you wouldn't have to go back to the export department. Once you've escaped the clutches of G Smith & Son, the world's your oyster. No one will be able to force you to return to the family business.'

Olivia had a point.

'I'll think about it,' Nancy said.

5

Nancy looked out of the office window across the factory's grey metal roof towards the electricity pylons that led her gaze to the grey bank of clouds floating over Coventry. Another dull, grey day, which was highly likely to be followed by plenty more. It was only one week into 1964, and she was already bored stiff. Could she really stick this out until September? There wasn't even enough secretarial work to keep her mind occupied this morning.

Her old boss had retired before Christmas, so now she had a new manager to train: Mr Jefferson. He was in his early 30s, and he'd seemed quite personable when they'd been introduced yesterday morning, although he had terrible taste in aftershave, which was unfortunate as he liberally dowsed himself in it. At least she didn't have to share an office with him. She'd overheard him spending most of yesterday afternoon on the telephone to various suppliers introducing himself. Based on the way he spoke, he obviously thought a lot of himself. But there was no sign of him this morning, which was odd as he hadn't had any meetings in his diary.

Nancy looked at the stack of manila folders on the end of her desk. Filing was the most boring part of her job, but she was sick of looking at the large pile of cardboard and paper. She picked up the folders and went over to the row of filing cabinets that lined the back wall of her office. She'd spend fifteen minutes returning them to their proper homes, then reward herself with a cup of tea.

The top folder was labelled "Twist & Co". She moved over to the end filing cabinet, opened the second drawer down and flicked through the tabs until she found the correct location.

She picked up the brown Manila folder and was just about to slip it into the drawer when she felt a hand on her left buttock. She tensed. The overwhelming smell of Old Spice gave her a big clue as to who the offender was.

'How about a drink at lunchtime?' a voice whispered in her ear.

She swung around, hitting Mr Jefferson with the folder and slamming the drawer shut as she leaned against the cabinet. He stepped back in surprise.

'No need for that, Nancy.'

'What do you mean, Mr Jefferson?' she asked in her most innocent voice.

'There's no need for the formality either. I've told you before you can call me Jim when no one else is around.'

He leaned over her, his right hand pulling her waist close against his body. The smell of stale cigarettes on his breath made her want to wretch.

She wriggled out of his grasp and hurried back to the safety of her desk.

He looked annoyed. 'I could arrange for you to move into the typing pool. You'd have no privileges there.'

'I think my father might have something to say about that,' she snapped back. Though right now, the typing pool was quite appealing. Working with ten other women would mean that Mr Jefferson would be unlikely to corner her alone again. There was a lot to be said for safety in numbers.

He sniggered. 'And what influence does your father have? Does he own the factory?' Mr Jefferson's easy charm had disappeared.

'Actually, yes.'

It was satisfying watching the patronising smirk disappear from his face and seeing the colour drain from his skin as she added, 'He is the son in G Smith and Son. I'm sure he'll be most interested to hear how my day went when we have family dinner this evening.'

Nancy busied herself assembling multiple sheets of paper and carbon paper, tapping them on the desk to align them and slipping them into the typewriter, ready to type a letter, all the time avoiding eye contact with Mr Jefferson.

'There's obviously been a misunderstanding. There's no need to mention this to your father,' he said, quickly walking out of the office.

Nancy sighed. It wouldn't have been like this if her parents had considered letting her go to Cambridge like her brother. She looked up at the ceiling, visualising walking across a sunlit quadrangle. *Too late for that, Nancy. Focus on getting the cash together to pay for your share of Patty's sailing project.* She might even be able to meet up with Billy when they docked in Sydney. She typed the letter while fantasising about lounging on Bondi Beach with Billy rubbing suntan oil on her back.

'All work and no play.' The familiar voice of Nancy's office neighbour, Bernie, brought Nancy back to reality. 'I'm going to walk into town at lunchtime. Do you want to join me?'

Bernie was the Works Manager's secretary. They had met when Bernie had been tasked with looking after Nancy in her first week. She was a couple of years older than Nancy, but they'd hit it off immediately. A lunchtime walk with Bernie would be far more entertaining than eating her cheese and pickle sandwiches alone in the office. 'You're on. I'll be finished in half an hour.'

Bernie reappeared at Nancy's office door five minutes early. 'Are you ready yet?' she asked. Judging by her big smile, she was bursting to tell Nancy something good.

Nancy grabbed her coat and handbag. 'Go on then. What's your news?' she asked as they walked down the stairs to the office's back door.

Bernie looked as excited as a puppy with a new tennis ball being dangled in front of its nose. 'Trevor asked me to marry him last night.'

Nancy wasn't surprised. Bernie had been going out with Trevor for well over a year and seemed to be besotted with him.

'And what did you say?'

'Yes, of course!' Bernie looked as if Nancy was insane to think she would've said anything else.

Nancy had never met Trevor, but Bernie had described him in great detail during the time Nancy had known her. Based on Bernie's updates, "reliable" and "conventional" were the two adjectives that sprang to mind - not Nancy's type at all. Though, as Nancy hadn't had a man in her life since she left Devon last summer, could she even claim to have a type?

'Did he go down on one knee?'

'Oh yes. We were outside the Odeon. We'd just watched *The Pink Panther*, and the rest of the cinemagoers gave us a round of applause. Aren't you going to say congratulations?'

Nancy had been thinking about the horror of getting married at twenty-three. She pictured Bernie in a couple of years' time, stuck at home with a bawling toddler and a baby on the way. But then Bernie was still living at home in a small three-bedroomed terrace with her parents and four younger siblings, so in those circumstances, Nancy might have been keen to escape too. Nancy wanted to see some of the world before she settled down.

'Sorry. Of course, I'm happy for you.'

'Trevor's suggesting we get married at Christmas.'

Nancy didn't like the way Trevor dictated everything he and Bernie did. 'And what do you think?' she asked.

'I think it's a marvellous idea. It will be nice to start 1965 as Mrs Foster. I do love the sound of that.' Bernie looked dreamy at the prospect.

'I hope you'll be very happy together.' Nancy said, trying to make up for her initial lack of enthusiasm.

'So when are we going to get you fixed up?' Bernie asked. 'I'm sure Alan in Accounts fancies you. I've seen how he looks at you when you walk along the corridor.'

Alan in Accounts was made from the same mould as Trevor - conventional looking in his neat suit, highly polished shoes, and Brylcreemed hair. He always wore the same thin sky-blue tie - a nod to Coventry City Football Club's latest football strip, no doubt. Nancy preferred someone more rugged. Her thoughts drifted to Billy and his extracurricular lessons around the back of the Dashford Sailing Club building. She suspected Bernie wouldn't approve. Nor would Alan.

'Nancy? Are you ok? You're looking quite flushed.'

'Sorry, I think I've got a cold coming on.'

'We better pop into Boots to get you some Beecham's powders.'

6

Nancy lay on her bed at home, flicking through the French phrase book she'd bought in town at lunchtime while Bernie was browsing the wedding planning manuals. She recognised more words and phrases than she thought. It shouldn't be too hard to get up to speed again. And, as Olivia had said, she was bound to learn more quickly in Paris. Nancy smiled to herself. *Let's face it, you're not going to learn anything new and exciting staying here. And Olivia's right - once you've got away from Coventry, escaping on that sailing trip will be much easier.*

The dinner bell rang downstairs. There was no time like the present. She'd raise it with her parents while they were tucking into overcooked lamb chops with peas and plain boiled potatoes, the meal they always ate on Tuesday evenings.

Nancy's father looked furious. 'Don't be so ridiculous. No daughter of mine is going to Paris on her own. It would ruin your reputation. What would the neighbours say?'

As far as Nancy was aware, he hadn't spoken to the neighbours for years. In the Smiths' large five-bedroomed detached house set in its own grounds on the outskirts of

Coventry, they didn't even see Mr and Mrs Clarke next door, let alone speak to them. She doubted he would lower himself to acknowledge their existence even if they danced naked across the front lawn.

'And you. You're strangely silent?' he shouted at Nancy's mother at the other end of the dining table. 'You should be backing me up on this.'

'I think it's a good idea,' his wife said calmly as she struggled to cut another tough piece of meat from her lamb chop.

'I'm sorry, what did you say?' her husband yelled.

She put down her knife and fork. 'I said I think it's a good idea. You want to expand the export department. Having someone you can trust who's fluent in French would be a boon. Nancy's only going for six months. Olivia's father has an agreement in principle with the bookshop owner. Plus, Olivia is there already. Nancy wouldn't be on her own.'

'It's alright for the upper classes like your family and the Forbes to swan around abroad. But it's not for my daughter.'

There it was - the enormous chip on his shoulder. Nancy's father had been a grammar school boy. Nancy's mother, on the other hand, had gone to a private girls' boarding school and grown up in a mansion in Devon. Her family hadn't always been wealthy. Nancy's great-grandparents had purchased Dashford Grange in 1886 using a generous financial gift from the then Prince Edward to keep Nancy's great-grandfather quiet while the Prince was having a torrid affair with Nancy's great-grandmother. However, one generation later, Nancy's grandmother chose to forget about her family's meteoric rise to the upper classes, acting as if they had been members of the landed gentry for centuries. She was very much of the opinion that her daughter had married beneath her station when Nancy's mother walked down the aisle with the son of a Midlands factory owner.

Nancy also wondered what her mother saw in her father, though in their wedding photo, he did look handsome in his wartime army uniform. It was difficult to believe that the slim, smiling man was the same person as the balding, red-faced lump of pure rage currently sitting at the end of the dining table.

'You were swanning around abroad at my age,' Nancy said in disgust.

'Swanning around! I was fighting the Nazis, I'll have you know, young lady.'

'There weren't many Nazis in the army stores, as I remember, dear,' Nancy's mother chipped in.

Nancy's father ignored his wife. 'I won't hear of it.'

He threw his napkin on the dining table and marched into the hall. They heard his heavy footsteps as he stomped across the parquet floor, followed by the slam of his study door.

'That went well,' Nancy said to her mother.

'He's had a bad day,' Nancy's mother sighed.

Nancy was furious. 'Please don't make excuses for him, Mother. I've had a bad day too. I'm going to Paris regardless of what he says.'

7

Six weeks later, after leaving a note for her mother and sneaking away from home at 4 am, Nancy walked out of the Porte Dauphine Metro station and into the unseasonably warm Parisian spring air. She sprang back from the edge of the road as a green frog-eyed 2CV rushed past, blowing its horn. That had been close. *Concentrate, Nancy! Otherwise, this is going to be the shortest trip you've made anywhere.*

She tried again, safely reaching the opposite pavement this time. She pulled the now ragged letter out of her coat pocket. Olivia had drawn a map of how to get from the station to her apartment at 27 Rue de la Dordogne. It should be just around the corner here. Nancy turned into a narrow street and headed uphill, counting the numbers until she arrived at a large brown door. An ornate brass Art Nouveau doorbell push was mounted on the yellow-painted plaster wall next to it.

Nancy pressed the bell. She heard a distant ringing sound, followed by a door slamming, then footsteps. The front door creaked open, and a 60-something woman peered around its edge. She must be Madame Morceau, the concierge that Olivia had mentioned in her letter.

'Oui?' the woman said.

At least Nancy understood that. 'I'm here to visit Olivia Forbes,' she said in her faltering schoolgirl French.

'Hmmm.' Madame Morceau opened the door wider to let Nancy into a small courtyard.

'Là,' she said, pointing to another brown door in the corner of the courtyard.

'Merci, Madame.'

Nancy staggered across the courtyard, pushed open the door the concierge had indicated and stepped into a dark hallway with some tatty stairs going up. Whoever had chosen the decor had been a fan of brown - the walls and the woodwork were all painted the same dull, muddy colour. Olivia had been right when she said it wasn't the Ritz.

Olivia's apartment was on the top floor. The stairs seemed to go on forever. Nancy's suitcase felt like it was getting heavier with each step. She was gasping for breath by the time she reached the top landing. She banged on the door. Please let Olivia be in.

'You look washed out,' Olivia's familiar voice said as she opened the door with a smile. 'I'll make some tea.'

'I'm so pleased to see you. It's been such a long day. I swear my arms are three feet longer than when I set out this morning. I've been lugging this bloody thing around for hours.' Nancy dumped her suitcase by the door and made straight for the sofa. 'Those stairs were the last straw,' she added as she took off her shoes and flopped down into the pile of cushions.

'You're here now. And you'll be running up and down those stairs easily within a week. It helps burn off the bread and cheese.'

'Bread and cheese?' Nancy had hoped they'd be eating something more interesting than bread and cheese.

'It is French bread and cheese - not a slice of Hovis and a lump of cheddar. That's all I can afford to eat most weeks,'

Olivia said as she went into the kitchenette area and put a kettle on to boil on the hob.

'I thought you said your job paid well?'

'It does, but I have a nasty habit of spending it on wine and clothes, not necessarily in that order.'

Nancy wasn't surprised. Olivia was always smartly dressed in the latest fashions, whereas Nancy preferred a more casual look. But she might have to up her game now she was here. She'd noticed that most of the women she'd encountered since landing at Charles de Gaulle airport looked much more stylish than she did.

The living room had two small windows, partially obscured by heavy curtains, which made it quite dark even though it was still broad daylight outside. 'If you're up to walking a few more steps, I'll show you around our stately home,' Olivia said.

Nancy reluctantly got up again.

'I'm through there.' Olivia pointed to an open door to another room with a double bed, a large wardrobe similar to the ones in Nancy's grandmother's mansion, and an ornate dressing table. 'And this one's yours.'

Nancy looked into a bedroom that was just big enough to hold the single bed pushed next to the window. She opened the door in the corner, which revealed a small closet.

'There's some space in my wardrobe if you're stuck.' Olivia sounded apologetic. 'But you have a great view if that's any consolation.'

Nancy knelt on the bed and opened the net curtains. Olivia was right. The top-floor window had a view across the local rooftops. In the distance, the Eiffel Tower broke the skyline - a picture postcard scene. She'd have to photograph it at some point, but she was too tired to get her camera now.

'Welcome to Paris, Nancy.'

The following morning, Nancy awoke to the sound of her alarm clock ringing on the floor beside the bed. At least the lack of space for a bedside table forced her to get out of bed to turn it off. She'd have much preferred to turn over and go back to sleep. She groaned as her stiff arms and shoulders objected to moving. She should've packed less. She headed across the living room to the bathroom. The sound of Olivia singing in French drifted through the door.

'Are you going to be long?' Nancy shouted.

'Five minutes. Make the coffee, will you.'

Nancy headed to the kitchenette area and looked around for a jar of Nescafe. There was no sign of one anywhere, but she did find a bag labelled 'café'.

She grabbed two coffee cups from the solitary wall cupboard, boiled some water in the kettle on the hob, and put a spoonful of coffee in each cup. Despite vigorous stirring, the coffee refused to dissolve properly. Perhaps the grains were supposed to settle.

She put Olivia's cup of black coffee on the dining table while she looked in the fridge for milk for her own. Olivia emerged from the bathroom.

'That's super, thank you.' She picked up the cup and took a gulp. She spluttered. 'Nancy, what did you do?'

Nancy explained.

Olivia laughed. 'It's not instant. You need the cafetière.'

'I need what?'

Olivia grabbed a glass jug with a chrome lid and a plunger. 'This. Didn't you have one at home?'

'No, I've never seen one of those before.'

'Watch and learn,' Olivia said as she put the coffee grounds inside the cafetière along with hot water from the kettle, then attached the lid. 'We leave it for four minutes to brew.'

'Isn't instant a lot easier?'

'Yes, but it doesn't taste as good.' Olivia disappeared into her room to get dressed while Nancy swilled away her failed coffee-making attempt.

'Should be ready now,' Olivia said, returning to the kitchenette. Nancy watched as she pushed down the plunger and poured the dark, hot liquid into the freshly washed cups. She handed one to Nancy.

Nancy took a tentative sip and grimaced. 'That's so bitter. I'll stick to tea. I assume there's no weird French device for making that?'

'No,' Olivia laughed, passing her a teapot and a jar labelled thé. 'Will you be alright going to the bookshop on your own? Madame Dubois wanted to get all her daily admin jobs done before she started training you today, so she's expecting you at half past ten, but I've got to be at work before that.'

'I'll be fine.' Nancy checked the new map that Olivia had drawn her last night. The bookshop was only three streets away.

Nancy went into her bedroom and returned, clutching a pair of trousers and a Crimplene dress. 'What should I wear?'

'Definitely the dress - stick to whatever you wore to the office at home. Technically, it's illegal for women to wear trousers here.'

'Seriously?'

'Seriously, though, I doubt you'd get arrested. I think it has more to do with stopping you from rebelling during the revolution.'

'I've been here less than 24 hours. I'll leave leading an uprising until at least next week, even if the coffee is awful.' Nancy laughed.

8

The bookshop was on a corner, exactly where Olivia said it would be. A sign waving in the wind on the wall outside advertised it in gilded Art Nouveau-style lettering as "Dubois's English Bookshop" with "Bespoke Bindings" in smaller, plainer capital letters underneath. Nancy walked up the steep steps to the front door and pushed it open. A bell tinkled, and a well-dressed woman in her early 50s peered over half-moon glasses at her from behind the counter at the rear of the shop.

Nancy smiled at her. 'Bonjour, madame. Je suis Nancy Smith.'

The woman looked at her wristwatch. 'Excellent! I adore staff who are punctual,' she said in perfect English. 'Madame Dubois,' she added, offering her hand for Nancy to shake. 'You don't have to speak French when you're here. I was born and raised in London. The French surname is courtesy of my late husband.'

She raised part of the counter to let Nancy into the back of the shop. 'Let me show you where to put your things, then I can give you a tour of our wonderful emporium. Philip, you're in charge for five minutes.'

Nancy followed Madame Dubois's gaze to see a large man in his late 20s unpacking a box of books in the far corner shop. He smiled and raised his hand. Nancy waved back.

Madame Dubois led the way through a door into a room that appeared to double as an office and a kitchen.

'Coat pegs are there.' Madame Dubois waved her hand in the general direction of a brown coat hanging in the corner. 'Put your bag in the cupboard underneath.'

Madame Dubois seemed welcoming enough, but something about her manner gave Nancy the impression that it was best to do as you were told. She opened the cupboard door and put her shoulder bag on the shelf.

'The toilet is out in the yard,' Madame Dubois said, opening the door so Nancy could look out. As soon as she did so, an animated ball of black fur shot into the kitchen.

'Oh, you have a cat,' Nancy said excitedly, bending down to stroke it.

'No, I don't!' Madame Dubois said firmly. 'Get out, you stupid animal.'

She used her foot to push the poor creature towards the open door. The cat took the hint and sauntered casually outside again.

'That was Mimi. She belongs to the café next door. Do not let her in under any circumstances. I'm allergic to cats.' She emphasised the point by sneezing loudly.

'Would you prefer tea or coffee?' Madame Dubois asked.

'Tea, please.' Nancy wanted to avoid a repeat of the coffee saga at breakfast.

'Excellent. A girl after my own heart.' Madame Dubois. 'Philip also prefers tea. He likes his strong with two sugars - obviously a builder in a previous life. I prefer my tea much weaker,' she laughed. 'But don't worry, you don't have to remember all of that because we have a chart.'

Madame Dubois pointed to a piece of paper taped to the cupboard over the sink. There were a lot of names on the list, but most of them were crossed out. Each person had a description of how they liked their hot drink accompanied by a tea or coffee stain, presumably to give whoever was making the drinks a visual guide to the strength they preferred.

'Cups are in the cupboard, along with sugar and tea. We don't leave the sugar out - the ants are appalling in the summer. If they get so much as a whiff of it, there will be a long column of them marching across the floor and up the cupboard before you know it.'

Madame Dubois grabbed the kettle from the hob and turned on the tap over the large sink. The water spluttered out in stops and starts.

'The plumbing can be a little temperamental,' she said, enthusiastically bashing the copper pipe with the heel of her hand. 'There,' she said triumphantly, 'It's fine now. It's rather like a man. You just have to know where to hit it to get it to cooperate.'

It was an interesting analogy. Nancy wondered whether she had used that approach on the late Monsieur Dubois.

'I'll leave you to make the tea. There are just the three of us today. Bring the cups to the counter when they're ready, and then I will show you your duties in the shop.'

So, this was going to be her place of work for the next six months. It would do. It was curious how many people had left, though. Nancy counted the crossed-out names while she waited for the kettle to boil. Seven. Mostly women, all of them coffee drinkers with English names. Nancy's taste for tea might give her an advantage here.

She found a tray by the sink, put the cups on it, and made a pot of tea. Pouring three different strengths of tea from the same pot at the same time was going to be an art, the most important part of which would be getting Madame Dubois's tea correct.

She concentrated on the task until the contents of all three cups looked the right colour, then carefully carried the tray of drinks into the shop.

Madame Dubois nodded approvingly and took a sip from her cup. 'Perfect, Nancy. You've passed the first test. Not everyone does. Philip, tea is ready, my darling.'

Philip appeared from behind a bookshelf and walked over to Nancy, offering his hand.

'Philip Mason,' he said.

His handshake was pleasantly firm.

'Lovely to meet you, Philip. I'm Nancy Smith.'

'Pleased to meet you, Nancy.'

A customer walked into the shop. A rather smart gentleman with a trilby hat, which he politely raised to them. 'Good morning,' he said.

'Monsieur Ferrier, how lovely to see you.' Madame Dubois offered him her hand, which he duly took and tenderly kissed. 'We don't normally get the pleasure of your company on a Tuesday.'

'No, but I have to visit my daughter in Lyons tomorrow, so I wondered if you might have time to see me now?' Monsieur Ferrier asked.

'But of course.' Madame Dubois lifted the counter to let him through. 'Philip, please show Nancy around the shop while I'm helping Monsieur Ferrier,' she said as she shut the office door.

'Is he a regular customer?' Nancy asked Philip when they were alone again.

Philip grinned. 'Oh yes. At least once a week.'

'He must be a keen reader if he warrants personal attention.'

'He's keen, alright, but I'm not sure how much reading he does if you get my drift.' Philip raised his eyebrows.

Nancy looked puzzled.

'Let's just say he's not here for Madame Dubois's book recommendations.'

'What else is he here for then?'

Philip looked uncomfortable. 'I expect you'll work it out soon enough.'

Nancy walked into the flat, slightly less out of puff than yesterday, but then she hadn't had her heavy suitcase to contend with today. Her toes were throbbing from standing up all afternoon, though. She shrugged off her coat, kicked off her shoes and put her feet up on the sofa. Bliss.

Olivia arrived home five minutes later. 'How did your first day go?' she asked as she hung up her coat in her bedroom.

'It was interesting. Madame Dubois is lovely, and her other assistant, Philip, is nice too.'

'Nice?'

'Not Billy's level of nice. I mean, he's quite a hunk. I think he must lift weights, but I don't fancy him. He showed me around the shop and how to work the till. He doesn't seem to be that into books, though. And there's something else odd, too.'

'What do you mean?'

'I might be working in a knocking shop.'

'What?'

'I think Madame Dubois might be a prostitute.'

'What on earth made you come to that conclusion?' Olivia sat down in the armchair next to the sofa.

'Four gentlemen visited the shop today, but none of them bought a book.'

'I'm sure that happens in all the bookshops in Paris, or anywhere else for that matter. How many times have you been into a bookshop just to browse?'

'Lots of times, but these customers didn't so much as look at the shelves. They just went straight out to the back of the shop with Madame Dubois, presumably into her personal quarters, because I made a point of going into the office just after the third one arrived, and there was no sign of either of them.'

Olivia looked serious. 'What sort of gentlemen?'

'They were all older men. The first one was a retired man in his mid-70s, I'd say, and the others were in their late 50s or early 60s, all smartly dressed. The first one didn't have an appointment. He usually visits on Wednesdays, according to Philip. But the others all had bookings from the way she greeted them. When each one arrived, Madame Dubois disappeared off with them, and within an hour, they were on their way out again.'

'She could be giving them personal book recommendations, or Tarot readings or something else innocent?'

'I wondered that. But that time I went into the office, I heard strange moaning noises coming from upstairs. And when Madame Dubois reappeared after that client left, she was wearing a completely different outfit to the one she had on before. Plus, we only had three people buy books today. The takings wouldn't have covered mine and Philip's salaries, let alone the cost of running the shop and feeding and clothing Madame Dubois.'

'Perhaps Tuesday is a quiet day.'

'Possibly. I'll let you know what happens tomorrow.'

Olivia drummed her fingers on the arm of the chair.

'You look worried,' Nancy said.

'I'm wondering how my father knows her now.'

9

Wednesday, Thursday and Friday at the bookshop continued in much the same vein as Tuesday: two or three male visitors for Madame Dubois each day and only a few book sales, though the shop had been busier with more customers coming in to browse. Nancy tried to quiz Philip on what he knew about Madame Dubois's gentlemen callers, but he kept changing the subject. Perhaps he didn't know any more than she did, or he did know and didn't want it to put her off. If Nancy's theory was correct, it might explain the high staff turnover.

Philip told her that he always took Saturdays off, which meant Nancy would have a new colleague tomorrow - someone called Carol, who Philip said came from Manchester and was studying French literature at the Sorbonne for a year. She hoped Carol might be more talkative on the subject of the mysterious men.

Olivia arrived home from work on Friday evening, clutching a bulging carrier bag with a baguette sticking out of the top.

'We have a party to go to tonight,' she announced as she took her key out of the lock.

Nancy perked up. Nice as Philip and Madame Dubois were, she could do with some social interaction with other people. 'Where is it?'

'At Christa and Ingrid's. They live across the road. They're German translators in the office next door to me. I think you'll like them. I've been to their parties before. They usually invite a good mix of interesting people. That's where I met Pierre. He'll be there this evening.'

'Count me in.' Nancy was intrigued by Olivia's latest boyfriend. She'd not mentioned him in her letters. From the little she'd said since Nancy had arrived, they'd only started seeing one another a few weeks ago. He was about 30 years old and some sort of artist - not Olivia's usual professional type at all. He'd been away all week, so tonight would be Nancy's first opportunity to meet him.

'Excellent!' Olivia said. 'We might find a Billy replacement for you.'

That could be a bonus. Nancy's resolve to remain single in Paris was starting to waiver. But based on this week's bookshop clientele, Nancy wasn't going to find a new lover there. 'Dress code?' she asked.

'There isn't one. Wear whatever you like.' Olivia started unpacking her shopping bag. 'I've got some more bread and cheese. I suggest we fill up on that before we go out. That should line our stomachs nicely. Christa and Ingrid are rather generous with their drinks. I've got some gin for us to take with us, too.'

'Not wine?' Nancy had noticed that Olivia always kept a bottle of white in the fridge.

'They've billed it as an international cocktail party, so you and I are expected to bring British drinks. I drew the line at beer.'

Later that evening Olivia took Nancy across the street to the modern block of flats where Christa and Ingrid lived.

'No stair climbing here,' Olivia said. 'They have a lift.'

She pushed the button for the second floor. Two minutes later, they walked out onto a bright white corridor with plush, green carpet.

'It's a lot more upmarket than our building,' Nancy said.

'The Germans must pay better - or they get a decent accommodation allowance.' Olivia led them to the door of apartment 2C and knocked.

A petite woman with dark hair tied in a high ponytail and wearing a bright red dress opened the door and gave them a beaming smile. 'Perfect timing, ladies. I've just mixed our first cocktail of the evening.'

'Nancy, this is Christa,' Olivia said.

'So lovely to meet you.' Christa welcomed them into her living room. 'How are you finding Paris, Nancy?'

'I haven't seen a lot of it yet.' Nancy smiled. 'Olivia's promised to show me the sights on Sunday.'

'Has she?' a deep voice said behind her. 'I was hoping she'd be spending the weekend with me.'

Olivia smiled seductively at the man who now had his arm around her waist. 'Nancy, meet Pierre.'

Judging by the wrinkles around his eyes and the sprinkling of grey hair at his temples, he was nearer 40 than 30. But he sported an impressive tan and stubble, and he looked quite fit. She could see why Olivia might find him attractive.

'Pleased to meet you,' he said, though the look in his eyes gave Nancy the impression that he wasn't pleased at all. 'I need to whisk Olivia away for a while. We have a lot of catching up to do.'

Olivia looked apologetically at Nancy but didn't resist as Pierre quickly led her across the living room and onto the balcony, shutting the door behind them.

'Pierre doesn't like to overdo the charm,' Christa said. 'Come on. I'll introduce you to everyone else, but first, you need a drink.'

Christa led Nancy past a few other guests in the spacious living room and into a large, modern kitchen. One of the work surfaces was covered in an assortment of bottles of various shapes and sizes.

'We bought gin with us, but Olivia's got it with her,' Nancy said apologetically.

'Don't worry,' Christa said. 'As you can see, we have plenty. We're starting with mojitos. Can I tempt you with one?'

'That would be lovely.' Nancy had no idea what a mojito was, but she was willing to give it a try. Christa picked up a jug of clear liquid and poured it over a large tumbler full of ice. She stirred it vigorously with a plastic stick, added a sprig of fresh mint and a straw, then handed it to Nancy.

Nancy eagerly sucked in a mouthful. It was confusing. It tasted of rum, but the rum she was used to at home was deep brown.

'Is there a problem?' Christa asked.

'No. It's delicious. I was just trying to work out what was in it.'

Christa reeled off the list of ingredients, including white rum. Who knew you could get that? Nancy had a feeling she was going to learn a lot this evening.

Nancy spent the first half an hour or so having an animated conversation about sailing and surfing with three attractive Californians who lived in the flat upstairs until Christa persuaded them to mingle with the rest of the guests.

Ingrid made an appearance an hour later, apologising for being late to her own party, which, judging by the ribbing she got from the other guests, was a regular occurrence. She was accompanied by a short, cheery, dark-haired man, who she introduced as her boyfriend, Dieter.

Olivia was monopolised by Pierre, who, as far as Nancy could tell, barely took his hands or lips off her all evening.

Christa, meanwhile, flitted from group to group, topping up glasses and snacks or offering fresh cocktails with recipes that seemed to get more complicated as the night wore on.

At one point, Nancy found herself stuck with an earnest PhD student who had just returned from Greece and was eager to share far too much detail about how the marble for the Parthenon had been carved out of the rock above Athens.

Christa swooped in on a rescue mission. 'Georges, Elise is dying to hear about your latest finds,' she said, nodding towards an unsuspecting woman relaxing with a cigarette on the balcony.

'Thank you so much,' Nancy said when Georges was out of hearing distance.

'My pleasure. You stay there. I'll be back with something you're going to adore.'

A couple of minutes later, she returned with an enormous martini glass full to the brim with bright blue liquid. A cocktail umbrella balanced precariously on the edge of the glass, with a maraschino cherry stopping it from falling in.

Nancy smiled. Olivia had been right. Nancy did like Christa and Ingrid. She'd also been right about their generosity with drinks. This was Nancy's fifth or possibly sixth cocktail. It was getting harder to keep count.

'I really shouldn't,' Nancy said, surprised by how much she was slurring now. She prided herself on being able to handle her drink, but Christa and Ingrid must have been more generous with their measures than she thought. She took a sip. It was delicious - orangey with only a hint of alcohol. Surely something so sweet wouldn't do any harm.

Olivia looked horrified as she swam into Nancy's blurry vision. 'Good god. You knocked that back in one.'

'Did I?' Nancy looked at the glass in her hand. How had it suddenly become empty?

'This isn't some of your homegrown Devon scrumpy,' Olivia whispered in her ear. 'There are probably at least three shots of vodka in that.'

'I'll have you know that scrumpy can be quite potent,' Nancy said, feeling affronted on behalf of West Country cider makers.

'There's potent, and there's potentially blinding. And Christa's cocktails fall into the latter category. I should've warned you. I'm sorry I was so busy with Pierre. I'm obviously too late now.' Olivia stood with her hands on her hips, looking thoughtful. Or at least Nancy thought she did. It was becoming very difficult to focus.

'I'm perfectly fine!' Nancy tried desperately to concentrate on Olivia's face. 'I'll just sit still for a few moments, and all will be well.' She closed her eyes.

'Apfelschnaps, ladies?' Ingrid asked.

Nancy opened her eyes again to see Ingrid with a tray of shot glasses filled with a clear liquid.

'Thanks, but no thanks,' Olivia replied.

'But I've never had Apfelschnaps,' Nancy protested.

'And you're not having it now.' Olivia sounded adamant about that. Nancy knew there was no point in arguing with her when she used that tone of voice.

'I think we should go back home so you can sleep off what you've drunk already,' Olivia suggested. 'Though how I'm going to manage to get you across the road and up four flights of stairs, I'm not quite sure.'

That was the last thing that Nancy remembered before drifting off into a strange dream about being dragged along a tarmac path by a horse and then falling into a soft white cloud, though it was baffling how you could fall into a cloud in the sky when you were lying on the ground.

10

When Nancy arrived at the bookshop the following morning, Madame Dubois looked her up and down, raised an eyebrow, and suggested that she tidy the books on the second floor. Nancy smiled appreciatively. Her head was throbbing, and sudden movement or loud noises were not what she needed this morning. An hour earlier, she hadn't been convinced that she would actually manage to get washed and dressed, let alone walk to work. The relative peace and quiet of the history section would be a perfect place to recover from last night's excesses.

She slowly climbed the stairs and walked through the archway into Floor 2's sales area. It was smaller than the lower floors. Nancy assumed that Madame Dubois's private rooms took up more space up here. The table of recommended books in the middle desperately needed tidying, but if she tried that now, she was sure her brain would explode through her eye sockets. It would have to wait until her hangover had eased sufficiently to allow her to look down without being in pain. Nancy headed for the bookshelves at the back of the room. She'd concentrate on sorting the books at eye level until the aspirin Olivia had given her at breakfast kicked in.

She had settled into rearranging the Ancient History section into alphabetical order when she heard a polite cough.

Nancy turned to see a tall man leaning casually against one of the bookshelves near the stairs. He looked amused. He was about Nancy's age, possibly a little older. It was difficult to be sure as he was dressed quite conservatively in a suit and tie. The suit didn't fit him very well, and his hair was unusually short. He wasn't a follower of fashion, obviously.

'Can I help you?' Nancy asked abruptly, put out that he seemed to find what she was doing entertaining.

'Possibly.' He gave her a lopsided grin and walked over to the table. 'I'm looking for a copy of *Bleak House*.'

His words were perfect, but he had an accent. Not French. Dutch maybe?

'Charles Dickens?' she asked.

'Yes. Is there another one?'

'No. I just wanted to make sure we were talking about the same book. I'm afraid you won't find it on this floor. It will be downstairs in classic fiction.'

'Perhaps you could show me.'

'Of course.' Nancy led the way down the stairs, concentrating hard to keep her head level. She could feel him looking at her as they walked down to the ground floor. It ought to feel creepy, but somehow it didn't. He grinned at her again as she pointed to the shelf near the shop's front door. 'Do I amuse you?' she asked him directly.

'I find you pleasing to look at.'

Nancy wasn't sure how she felt about that, though as she'd only spoken a few words to him, he was hardly going to say it was her witty repartee that attracted him. With his sparkling blue eyes and strong jawline, Nancy was finding him pleasing to look at too.

'You don't remember me, do you?' he said.

'No. Should I?' Nancy was puzzled that she couldn't recall him at all. She prided herself on having an excellent memory for faces.

'I'm somewhat disappointed that you don't.'

Nancy tried to concentrate. He carried on before she could reply. 'I was at Ingrid and Christa's party last night.'

Oh God. He must have turned up after she had downed that lethal blue cocktail. 'Were you? I don't remember seeing you there.'

'We had a conversation about horses while I was helping your friend to get you back to your apartment.' He looked slightly abashed.

That explained it. Nancy had no recollection of how she'd ended up back in her own bed. She'd assumed Olivia had guided her there alone, but it sounded as if she'd needed help.

'I'm afraid I don't remember much at all after Christa's rather generous cocktails.'

'I'm pleased to see you've recovered,' he said. 'Mostly,' he added as she winced when the shop door slammed shut behind a customer on their way out.

'I underestimated how strong some of the drinks were. I assume you didn't.'

'No, I don't usually drink,' he said.

'That's very sensible. I should probably give it up, too.' Nancy felt uncharacteristically flustered in his presence. 'Let's see if we can find *Bleak House* for you,' she said, changing the subject. 'It should be here.'

She headed towards the shelf of Victorian novels. They looked at the spines together. Now he was standing close to her, she could smell him, too. No aftershave, but a pleasant manly smell mixed in with soap. It reminded her of Billy. *No, don't think about Billy.* She started to feel a warm glow in all the right places.

'I can't see it,' he said.

'Neither can I. It looks as if we've sold out.'

'Perhaps you could order me a copy?'

'Yes, of course. Follow me.' The warm glow had been getting stronger - Nancy was glad of the opportunity to move away from him. She headed for the cash desk.

'Everything ok?' Madame Dubois asked.

'Yes,' Nancy replied. 'This gentleman would like to order a book.'

Madame Dubois smiled. Usually, she dealt with any customer admin, but today, she handed Nancy the order book. 'I need to make a phone call. You can deal with it, Nancy,' she said, turning around and heading to the back of the shop before Nancy could object.

Damn. Filling out the order form would require her to look down, which was still going to be painful. Nancy was going to have to tough it out.

There were three sheets for every order: the customer copy on top, the warehouse copy underneath and finally, the bookshop copy at the bottom, which remained in the book. She knew how odd it must look as she peered down her nose, trying to get the flimsy blue sheets of carbon paper in position without tilting her head forward.

'Would you like me to do that?' the man offered.

He must think she was a fool. 'No, I'll manage, thank you.'

The throbbing pain was so intense it made her feel sick. She took a deep breath in a bid to make the nausea go away.

'Perhaps if I wrote my name and phone number for you,' he said.

Nancy gratefully handed him the book and pen. He neatly printed his details and handed it back to her.

She glanced at what he'd written. Hans Schmidt. That sounded German rather than Dutch.

'We share the same surname,' Nancy said.

'You're German?' Hans looked puzzled.

'Nein,' Nancy replied, using one of the few German words she knew. 'I meant I have the English equivalent.' *Why are you telling a complete stranger your name?*

'Of course, I understand,' he nodded. Nancy was jealous of his ability to move his head so painlessly.

She managed to fill out the book title, but finding the price in the catalogue was going to be more challenging. She felt around under the counter for it. It should be the thickest book. She was in luck - it was on the top of the pile. She pulled it out without bending her neck, hoping that nothing was on top of it, then gently put it down on the counter. Mission accomplished. But how was she going to look through the long lists of books without learning forward? Fortunately, Hans sensed her dilemma. 'Shall I look for you?'

'That would be very kind.' She eased the catalogue across the counter towards him. 'The fiction section is at the back. The books are listed alphabetically by author's surname.'

Hans efficiently flicked through the catalogue and found the entry for the paperback edition of *Bleak House*. He held it up at Nancy's eye height, pointing to the catalogue number and the price.

'Thank you so much.' She smiled in relief. He smiled back.

The order form was complete now. Thank god that was over. There was just the loud ring of the till to deal with when she took his payment. He produced his wallet, counting out the exact money in francs. At least she wouldn't have to worry about getting the correct change out of the till drawer.

'Merci beaucoup, Nancy,' he said as she handed him the top copy of his order. 'You will give me a telephone call?'

That was a bit forward. She liked the look of him, but expecting her to call him was presumptuous.

'When the book arrives,' he clarified, looking amused again.

Of course. *You stupid woman, Nancy!* 'If it's in stock at the warehouse, it usually takes two to three working days to arrive, a little longer if they have to order it in. We'll phone you when it's here. Is that an office number or your home number?' she asked. 'Just so we know when to phone,' she added in case he thought she was prying.

'Home. But you can always knock on my door in the evening.' He grinned again. 'I live in the apartment below yours.'

'Oh. I'm surprised I haven't seen you.'

'I'm out working a lot. I'm sure we will bump into one another on the stairs eventually.'

'Yes, I'm sure. I'll be in touch.'

'I shall look forward to that. Auf Wiedersehen, Nancy.'

'Auf Wiedersehen, Herr Schmidt,' she said, her eyes drawn to his pert backside as he walked confidently out of the shop.

'How are you feeling now?' Olivia asked as Nancy walked into the apartment.

'A lot better, thank you,' Nancy said as she removed her shoes. 'Though it would be difficult to feel much worse than I did first thing.'

'It definitely looked that way at 8 o'clock this morning. I'm impressed you managed a whole day at work.'

'Madame Dubois took pity on me and gave me light duties.' Nancy hung her coat on the back of her bedroom door.

'Did you manage to talk to the Saturday girl?'

'Carol? A little, once the worst of my hangover was over but she knows nothing. Madame Dubois didn't have any special visitors today. And even if she had, I doubt Carol would have noticed. She spent more time with her head in a book than doing any actual work.'

Nancy sat down on the sofa. 'Something interesting did happen today, though. Something you might be able to shed some light on.'

'Tell me more.' Olivia handed Nancy a cup of tea.

'Did a German man help you to get me home last night?'

Olivia grinned. 'So you do remember something. Yes, the lovely Hans. He and Pierre helped carry you back home. Don't worry. They were both perfect gentlemen when it came to getting you into the apartment.'

'He said he lives downstairs?'

'Yes, he does with his friend Dieter. Surely you remember Dieter and Ingrid last night?'

'Yes, I remember them arriving late, but not Hans. After drinking that lethal blue cocktail, the rest of the night was just a blur, but he came into the bookshop this morning.'

'How did he know you worked there?'

'I've no idea. Perhaps he didn't. I thought he was rather nice, though,' Nancy said, trying to sound casual.

'Billy's level of nice?' Olivia's interest was piqued.

'Possibly. He had the same twinkle in his eye. But I'm not getting involved with anyone here, remember.'

Olivia raised her eyebrows. 'Are we going to have to work out a system to notify one another if we have a guest?'

'Why? Are you about to give in to Pierre's attentions?'

'Who says I haven't already?' Olivia grinned.

'What, last night?'

Olivia pulled a face. 'It won't be happening again. It turns out not all Frenchmen are fantastic lovers.'

'Was it bad?'

'Let's just say one of us enjoyed it, and it wasn't me.'

'That's lousy.'

'Well, he was pretty drunk, but all the same. So what about Hans, then? Will you look into his twinkling eyes again? I gather they often twinkle for Christa.'

'What does that mean?'

'He's got the hots for her. Takes her out for expensive meals. But the feeling's not reciprocated.'

'Why does she go out with him then?'

'Free food.' Olivia looked in the kitchen cupboards. 'Perhaps you should make a play for him because we're still on bread and cheese until payday next week.'

'And what about Christa?'

'As I said, she's not that bothered about him. I don't think she's going to throw you in the Seine like some scorned lover.'

Nancy shook her head. 'If Hans has got the hots for Christa, I'm not getting involved. I don't need a cheater. There are plenty of attractive men around if I do decide to give in to my baser urges.' Though she had to admit, Hans was the first one who'd had the same effect on her as Billy.

Olivia wasn't going to be persuaded to give up on the idea that easily. 'But he came to see you at the bookshop.'

'He wanted to order a book. It's not that surprising.'

'A German wanting a book written in English when he lives in France. That's unusual, I'd say.'

Especially as, despite wanting a fiction book, he'd walked upstairs to the history section. *Don't read too much into that!* Nancy decided not to share that with Olivia either. 'His English might be better than his French? Perhaps it's for work.'

'I'm sure Christa said he's a biologist working for a research agency. What did he want to buy?'

'Bleak House.'

'Unless he is researching English social history in his spare time, I'd say that was very unusual.'

'It's good to have a hobby.'

'So, will you be seeing him again?'

'Not in that way. But I'll have to contact him when the book arrives.' Nancy was surprised at how happy she felt at the prospect.

11

'Nancy!' Madame Dubois called from the back room. 'Come in here, please.'

Nancy put down the box of books she was carrying and headed to the back of the shop. Madame Dubois smiled at her as she walked in from behind her desk. 'This morning's delivery had the book your customer ordered. Perhaps you'd like to call him,' Madame Dubois said, indicating the big black 1930s-style phone on the desk. 'I'll be out in the shop,' she said, winking at Nancy as she left.

Was she matchmaking, too? Olivia had asked several times over the last few days whether the book had arrived yet.

The order book was on the desk, open at Hans' order.

Nancy picked up the receiver. The dial tone sounded different to the one she was used to at home. She took a deep breath and dialled the number. It rang and rang. No reply. She felt strangely disappointed. But it was the middle of the morning on a weekday. Hans was most likely at work doing whatever biologists do, not that she knew what that could be. Did he work in a lab? Did he roam the shrubberies of Bois de Boulogne looking for insects? Perhaps he worked in a zoo. Did Paris even have a zoo? She hoped it didn't. Seeing animals locked up in cages always upset her.

She headed out into the shop again.

'When is Herr Schmidt coming in to pick up his book?' Madame Dubois asked.

'I don't know. I couldn't get through.'

'That's a shame. Try again after lunch.'

'I know where he lives, so I could deliver it.'

'Even better! I always like to exceed my customers' expectations. Is it far?'

'No. Only a few streets away, very near my flat.'

'Excellent. You must take it with you when you finish this evening.'

Nancy left work promptly, clutching *Bleak House* neatly wrapped in plain brown paper and tied up with red satin ribbon, which Madame Dubois had conjured up from somewhere in the depths of her desk drawer. She had tucked a business card under it, which Nancy studied on the way home. "Bespoke bindings for the discerning customer" was embossed on one side, with the shop phone number printed in black underneath. On the other side, Madame Dubois had written. "Thank you for your order. If we can help you with any of your binding needs, please pop in again."

It was an odd thing to write. Nancy hadn't really thought about the "bespoke bindings" aspect of the business since the day she saw it mentioned on the sign outside the shop. As far as Nancy was aware, all the books they supplied were standard ones unless Madame Dubois's appointments with her gentleman callers were to do with recovering old books. She'd not considered that as an option, though it was more realistic than the brothel theory. None of them had left with a book-sized parcel yet, though. She'd have to ask Madame Dubois when she returned to work tomorrow.

The sky had clouded over. It looked like it was about to rain, which was a shame because when Nancy had left the house this morning, Paris had been bathed in glorious sunshine, and she'd confidently stepped outside without bothering to take a coat. Judging by the state of the pavements, it had rained earlier this afternoon too. She started walking as fast as she could. *Bad clothing choice, Nancy - there's no chance of running in this pencil skirt.*

As she turned the corner into the next street, large raindrops began to spatter the pavement. Great! It wasn't just a shower, it was going to throw it down. Nancy picked up her pace with her head down as the rain became heavier. She tucked Hans' book under her jumper, unconvinced that the brown paper would be enough to protect it from a downpour.

A car sped past, spraying her with water from a large puddle in the gutter. She looked down at the muddy spots that were now all over her pale blue skirt. It was going to have to go to the dry cleaners now. Where even was the nearest dry cleaner? She'd have to consult Olivia when she got home.

By the time Nancy arrived at number 27, she was soaked. She opened her handbag to get out her keys, but they weren't there. It was only a small bag, so how could they be hidden? Then she remembered taking the rubbish downstairs before she left for work this morning. She'd put the keys in her coat pocket so she could get back in the apartment, but, of course, the coat was now hanging on the back of a dining chair inside. Marvellous. What a perfect day. She rang the bell.

Madame Morceau opened the door immediately. Wrapped up in a hat and coat, she looked as if she was on her way out.

'I forgot my keys,' Nancy explained in English, struggling to recall what the French for keys was.

Madame Morceau looked Nancy up and down disgustedly, then she stood back to let her in. She turned and slammed the door shut after herself without offering Nancy any further help. *Let's hope Olivia is back from work. If she isn't, you're going to be stuck outside in your dirty, sodden clothing.*

Nancy ran across the courtyard to the stairs and stood dripping in the small hallway. She wiped her hand across her face to stop the water running off her nose. She looked at the bump under her jumper. Her original plan had been to drop the book off with Hans on the way upstairs, but there was no way she wanted him to see her in this state. She'd have to pop down with it later after she'd dried off and got changed.

She climbed the stairs to the top floor and knocked on the apartment door. There was no reply. 'Olivia!' Nancy shouted through the door. 'I forgot my keys.' She banged more stridently this time. Still no reply.

'Can I help?' a familiar voice behind her asked.

She turned to see Hans standing at the top of the stairs. He had that slightly amused expression again. 'Herr Schmidt,' she said.

'Hello, Nancy. Please call me Hans. I heard you banging on the door.'

'I forgot my keys.'

'Madame Morceau should be able to let you in.'

'She was on her way out when I arrived.'

'Oh,' he said.

'But Olivia should be back from work any moment now.' Nancy shivered, realising the rain had soaked through to her underwear. It felt clammy against her skin now that she was standing still.

'You will catch a cold like that,' he said, looking concerned.

She smiled, trying to make light of the situation, though inside, she was cursing her bad luck. This was only the third time that Hans had met her, and yet again, she was in some form of distress. Even if she had wanted to start going out with him, there was no way those feelings would be reciprocated now. 'I do feel a little like a drowned rat.'

'Or some other animal,' he grinned.

What did he mean by that? Another droplet of water ran down her nose and dripped onto the floor.

'You are welcome to wait in my flat until Olivia comes home,' Hans offered.

'Thank you.' There was nothing to lose.

Hans led the way down to the third floor and invited her in. The apartment had a similar layout to Olivia's but with higher ceilings and taller windows, making the living room much brighter. It was neatly but sparsely furnished. Nancy's gaze was drawn to the dining table. It looked as if Hans had been eating a snack.

'Sorry! I've disturbed your meal.'

'Not at all. I was just finishing.' He walked over to the fireplace, turned on the two-bar electric fire then pulled one of the armchairs close to it. 'This will help dry you off,' he said.

'I might make your chair soggy.'

'Soggy?'

'It means damp, from my wet clothes.' she explained.

'Oh, I see. I have a solution to stop you from making it soggy. Just a moment.' He disappeared into what Nancy guessed must be the bathroom and returned with two fresh towels. He handed one to her. 'For drying your hair,' he said. Then neatly refolded the other to make it fit perfectly across the seat and the back of the chair. 'There. You can sit now without fear of making it soggy.'

Nancy sank into the armchair, feeling grateful for the warmth of the fire as she watched its bars glow steadily more orange. She dried her hands on the towel, then dabbed her face with it.

'I was going to pop down to see you anyway,' she said, 'I've got your book.' She carefully removed the parcel from under her jumper.

'Thank you for delivering it.' Hans looked at the card. He appeared as puzzled by the message as Nancy had been.

'Have you any need for bespoke bindings?' Nancy asked.

'No. It's a very, how do say, niche market.'

'One that seems to appeal to older men.'

'What makes you say that?'

It felt a bit gossipy, but she'd have to say something now. 'It's just that Madame Dubois's bespoke clients seem to be men who are over 50.'

'I expect it's an expensive service. Are there many of them?'

'A few a day.'

Hans looked thoughtful. She decided to change the subject. 'I'm curious. Why *Bleak House*?'

'I'm trying to improve my English. Charles Dickens is one of your greatest writers, and it is supposed to be his finest book. Have you read it?'

'No. I had enough of Dickens at school. Far too wordy for my tastes.'

'Who would you recommend I read?' Hans was sitting in the opposite armchair now.

'I'm enjoying the latest John Le Carré. *The Spy Who Came In From The Cold.*'

Hans looked thoughtful. 'I have heard of it. But it is not, how do you say, my cup of tea. Which reminds me, I'm forgetting my manners. Would you like a coffee?'

'Have you got any tea? I'm not really a coffee drinker. It's too bitter for my taste.'

'Well, you haven't drunk my coffee before. And I'm sorry we haven't any tea. Can I offer you a glass of water instead?'

'I think I've had enough water today, one way or another.'

Hans laughed. 'I will make you a coffee to try. I won't be offended if you don't like it.'

He headed to the kitchenette.

'No Dieter today?' Nancy asked.

'No. He went to Ingrid's.'

'You're not visiting Christa?' *Stop fishing, Nancy!*

'No, she didn't want to see me today. I don't think she wants to see me most days.' He laughed awkwardly

'So why do you keep asking her out?'

'I don't know, ' he hesitated. 'Perhaps I am an optimist.' He went quiet while he concentrated on putting the coffee filter in the percolator.

It was obviously a sensitive subject, which was understandable as his feelings weren't being reciprocated. Time to talk about something else. 'How long have you lived in Paris?

'Just over a year.'

'And what do you do here?'

'I'm in import-export.'

'Olivia thought you were a biologist.'

'Dieter is the biologist. What did you do before you came to Paris?'

'I worked for my father's business as a secretary.' That seemed a lifetime away now.

'Did you enjoy it?'

She could easily spend a full half an hour explaining why she didn't enjoy it, but she decided not to bore him with the details. 'No. I'm not cut out for office work. It was far too monotonous. I prefer something more adventurous.'

'Like working in a bookshop?' He gave her that attractive grin again.

'Cheeky,' she said. 'It's a means to an end. I get to see a little more of the world while I save to go travelling a lot further away.'

'Where are you going to next?'

'On a round-the-world sailing trip, then possibly Australia.'

'That's a long way to go. Do you know anyone in Australia?'

It was Nancy's turn to hesitate now. 'No. How about you? How long will you stay in Paris?'

'For a few more months at least.'

'And where's home?'

'Berlin.'

'It must be peculiar living in a city that's split in two.'

'Yes, it is. Though I haven't spent a lot of time there since the wall was built. Where's home for you?'

'Coventry. That's where I grew up, but Devon is the place I feel most at home.' She went on to tell him about Dashford-on-Sea and spending her childhood summer holidays at her grandmother's grand house.

'That explains why you want to go sailing.'

'Yes, I love being out at sea. The wilder the weather, the better.'

He returned with her coffee. 'Try this.'

Nancy tentatively took a sip. It was quite pleasant. 'Actually, it's not bad. Thank you.'

'I'll take that as a compliment. It's a milder roast than you usually get in France, and I add warm milk. Have I converted you to being a coffee drinker?' He settled back into the other armchair.

'I wouldn't say that, but it's a lot better than the coffee Olivia makes.'

Nancy heard footsteps upstairs. 'Talk of the devil. It sounds like she's home.'

Hans frowned. 'I thought you and Olivia were best friends?'

'Oh, we are. "Talk of the devil" means you've been talking about someone, and then they coincidentally appear.'

Hans smiled. 'I understand now. I will have to remember that.'

'I better go. Thank you again,' she said, finishing the coffee.

'My pleasure. Thank you for improving my English.'

Nancy thought for a moment. She'd like another conversation with Hans. 'Perhaps I can help you improve your English again?'

He smiled. 'I would like that. I'll consult my diary later and let you know when I'm free.'

'Where have you been?' Olivia asked as she opened the apartment door to Nancy.

'I could say the same to you. You're usually back well before now.'

'You look like a forlorn panda.'

'What do you mean?'

'I think you need to check your face in the mirror,' Olivia said with a chuckle.

Nancy walked into the bathroom. Good god! Olivia was right. Thanks to the rain, her mascara had made a bid for freedom and was now covering the skin under her eyes and her cheeks with gungy black streaks. It looked like she'd smeared it around in big circles while she was drying off her face at Hans' earlier. *And you sat talking to him looking like that!*

'I got caught in the storm,' she said as she washed the mess off.

'You don't say. Did you finish work late today?'

'No. But I couldn't get in because I left my keys here.' Nancy headed over to the dining table and checked her coat pocket. There they were. She put them back in her bag. 'Were you working late today?'

'No. I went for a stroll in the Bois de Boulogne with Pierre.'

'Pierre?' What was Olivia doing back with that waste of space? 'I thought you'd dumped him.'

'I had, but he persuaded me to give him a second chance.'

'How did he manage that?'

'He sent me a gorgeous bouquet of roses at work. He's invited me to his family's chateau as well for Easter Sunday and who can resist a chateau.'

That explained it. Olivia had always preferred men with means. 'Where's that?'

'In the Loire Valley. He'll inherit it eventually.'

'So you can forgive him for being selfish in bed, provided you get to play Lady of the Manor in twenty years' time?'

'You make me sound so mercenary! Anyway, it's not just a chateau. He'll inherit the vineyard as well.'

12

'There's a note for you,' Olivia said to Nancy when she got up on Tuesday morning. 'Hand delivered.' She raised her eyebrows.

Nancy picked the envelope from the dining table. The handwriting was vaguely familiar. She ripped it open.

Dear Nancy

If your kind offer of an English lesson still stands, are you available after work today? The weather forecast says it will be a lovely evening. We could go for a walk in the Bois de Boulogne. I can meet you at the bookshop. Leave me a note if you can.

Yours

Hans

Olivia looked at Nancy expectantly. 'Well?'

'Well, what?'

'Who's it from?'

There was no point in teasing her any longer - Olivia had a knack for extracting information from anyone if she really wanted to. 'A certain Herr Schmidt.'

'Told you he fancied you.'

'You said no such thing.'

'Didn't I? I'm sure I did. I could tell from the way he treated you when you were drunk.'

'I very much doubt he fancies me. He just wants an English lesson.'

'Are you sure? His English sounded very good to me.'

'It is, but he wants to learn more.'

'And what sort of words are you planning to add to his vocabulary?' Olivia grinned.

'Not what you're thinking. I'll have to see what he wants to learn.'

Nancy had spent the afternoon working upstairs in the shop's history section again. She checked her watch. It was ten minutes before closing time. She'd left Hans a note under his door on her way out this morning, saying that giving him an English lesson was the least she could do after he'd helped her out last week, and she'd meet him outside the bookshop at 5.10 pm. She was hoping he'd read it.

Philip popped his head around the corner of the door to the stairs. 'Your favourite customer is here,' he said, grinning.

'Who?'

'The German fella. I didn't realise you were seeing him.'

'I'm not. He just wants an English lesson.'

'Is that what they call it now?'

'Don't you start. I get enough teasing from Olivia.'

'He's a handsome bloke. I wouldn't say no.'

From the few comments he'd made about what he got up to at weekends, Nancy had suspected Philip preferred men, but she hadn't expected him to be so open about it.

He misinterpreted her reaction. 'I'm sorry. I shouldn't have said that.'

'Don't apologise. I'm used to it being kept secret, that's all. Aren't you worried about being arrested?'

'Why do you think I prefer living in France? The French are a lot more tolerant than the English.'

'That must make life easier. But hands off Hans.' She was surprised at how jealous the thought of Hans being with someone else made her feel.

'So you do fancy him?' Philip said.

'Possibly,' she smiled. There was no possibly about it, but she was going to stick to her guns about not getting involved with someone. This was just an English lesson. Nothing more. *You don't want a repeat of the heartbreak you felt over Billy.*

'I'll finish up here. You go and see your beau.'

'Thank you.' She gave Philip a peck on the cheek and turned to head down the stairs just as Hans appeared.

'Hello, Nancy.'

'I was expecting to meet you outside,' she said.

'Sorry. I forgot you wrote that.' He didn't give Nancy his usual smile. She wondered how much he'd overheard.

Philip picked up some books that didn't need moving and headed to the shelves at the back of the shop floor. 'See you tomorrow,' he said.

'Yes, see you,' Nancy replied. She turned to Hans. 'I just need to get my bag, then we can go.'

He nodded and followed her downstairs. A few minutes later, they were on the street outside the shop.

'Which way?' Nancy asked.

'That direction will get us to the park the quickest,' Hans said, leading her across the road and down a side street. They carried on in silence for a few minutes. It was starting to feel awkward.

'Are you ok, Hans?' Nancy asked.

'I'm sorry I'm quiet. I have had a strange day,' he said. 'I think my manager would like me to return to Germany.'

'Oh!' Nancy attempted to hide her disappointment. 'Why's that?'

'She is not happy with my results. Is that the right word?'

'What sort of results are you talking about?'

'It is complicated. I'm sorry I mentioned it. Tell me about your day. It will take my mind off my problems.'

'I'm not sure it will. It hasn't been very interesting. Just a usual Tuesday at the bookshop.'

They crossed another road into the Bois de Boulogne.

'Has Madame Dubois had any special visitors today?'

'Yes, three. Two I've seen before, and one new man, who looks like he enjoys his food, shall we say.'

'Why?'

'I was trying to be polite.'

'Oh, I see.'

'He had an interesting surname. Monsieur Onkelinx. It didn't sound very French to me, but he sounded fluent when he was talking to Madame Dubois.'

'He might be Belgian?'

'Possibly. Anyway, this is not helping your English.'

'No, this is true. Would you like to sit down over there?' Hans said, pointing to a cafe by the lake. 'You must want to rest after spending all day on your legs.'

'Feet,' Nancy said.

'I'm sorry?'

'It would sound better if you said "spending all day on your feet".'

'I see. My lesson has started already,' he grinned.

At least she'd somehow cheered him up.

'That was a long walk,' Olivia said, when Nancy returned home later. 'How much vocabulary did you get through?'

'Nothing adventurous. We spent most of the time in a café, talking about our childhoods. He told me about his life in Germany during the war. It's so sad. He hasn't got any family left now. He was the only one to survive an air raid.'

'That must be tough. Still, no in-laws for you to worry about.'

'Olivia!'

'It's true. I'm quite nervous about meeting Pierre's family.'

'It shouldn't matter if they don't like you. Is Pierre the type of man who would ditch you if his parents' objected?'

'I'm not sure. I guess we'll find out in a couple of weeks. Anyway, when are you seeing Hans next?'

'He's meeting me after work again tomorrow.'

'He sounds keen.'

'Only because he wanted to check what some of the phrases meant in *Bleak House*, and he forgot to bring the book with him today.'

Olivia raised her eyebrows. 'That's convenient.'

It had crossed Nancy's mind that Hans might be using it as an excuse to see her again, but today had been a perfectly pleasant chat with no hint of him being attracted to her. She didn't want Olivia poking her nose in and ruining what could be a good friendship. 'I'm not getting involved with anyone here, remember,' she said.

13

It was Nancy's first Saturday off. Olivia had promised to show her around the sights of central Paris, but apart from a quick look at Notre Dame, the trip was turning into a guided tour of the best dress shops.

'You said you wanted to up your game fashion-wise,' Olivia said when Nancy complained.

'Yes, but I haven't budgeted for a new frock this month. I'm fine with the ones I've got.'

'Just one more shop, then we'll call it a morning,' Olivia said as they walked up to a rather chic boutique.

The sales assistant greeted Olivia with delight. 'It's so lovely to see you again. Do sit down. We've had some new styles in this week which I'm sure you will love,' she said, heading towards a rail at the back of the shop.

'How many dresses have you bought from here before?' Nancy whispered, 'Because I swear I saw the Franc signs appear in her eyes the minute she saw you.'

'One or two, possibly three.' Olivia looked sheepish. Nancy guessed that meant at least six.

'This dress is exactly your style,' the assistant said, returning with a shot silk dress in emerald green.

'It's beautiful.' Olivia looked besotted with it.

'Shall I put it in the changing room for you?' the assistant asked.

'Yes, please. I'll just see if there's anything else I like.' Olivia got up and started flicking through the hangers on the nearest rail.

'This blue one would look fabulous on you,' Olivia said, pulling out a dress with a fitted skirt and holding it up for Nancy to admire.

It was a pretty colour, similar to the large ocean blue topaz ring her mother loved to wear. Nancy got up and took the dress to the mirror. She held it against herself. The shape would be flattering. Perhaps she could skip the savings for another week.

'I'm sure Hans will find you irresistible in it,' Olivia said with a cheeky grin.

'Stop matchmaking. I don't want Hans to find me irresistible. He's good company, but there's no point in getting involved when I'll be leaving in a few months.'

Olivia looked amused. 'If you call going for coffee with him every evening after work, not getting involved.'

'We just chat, that's all.'

Nancy checked the price tag and gasped. 'We're going be on bread and cheese for the rest of the year if you buy a dress from here.' She quickly returned it to the rail.

'Don't exaggerate!' Olivia laughed. 'Only a couple of months, I'd say.' She disappeared behind the changing cubicle curtain. 'I haven't got much choice. I can't turn up to Pierre's family chateau in last year's fashions, can I?'

Nancy rolled her eyes. 'You haven't got your hands on the vineyard income yet. How would anyone tell if you wore one from last year?'

Olivia stuck her head around the changing room curtain. 'His mother is a former model. She'll notice. I need to create a good first impression.'

Surely Pierre's mother wouldn't care. But Olivia had decided she needed a new frock, and Nancy knew better than to argue.

Fifteen minutes later, they emerged from the boutique with Olivia carrying a large bag containing not one but two dresses. 'I'll need to get changed for dinner,' Olivia had reasoned. They headed in the direction of the Seine.

'Let's have a break for coffee,' Olivia said.

'A break?' Nancy said. 'How many more dresses do you need?'

'None, you'll be pleased to know. But I do need new shoes. I haven't got any that will go with these,' she said, looking at the shopping bag. 'Let's refuel first. We'll head for that café over there. They had a rather nice waiter last time I went in.'

Nancy didn't object. Offering opinions on the countless dresses Olivia had tried on this morning had proved to be surprisingly exhausting. A drink and a croque monsieur would do nicely.

The only snag was the café was at the other end of the street, and they'd have to walk past several shops to get there. Nancy had her fingers crossed that none of them was a shoe shop or another clothing boutique. She was willing to abandon Olivia if she so much as looked in another shop window. But it turned out to be Nancy's turn to get distracted. There was a newsagent just before the café, and the photo on the front of one of the newspapers caught Nancy's eye.

'Why have we stopped?' Olivia said.

'It's annoying, isn't it,' said Nancy. 'I recognise that man.'

'Which one?'

'This one.' Nancy picked up the newspaper and pointed to a thin gentleman of about 55.

'Who is he?'

'I know him as Monsieur Lambert or Mr Wednesday at 3 pm,' Nancy said, raising her eyebrows.

'Ooh. One of Madame Dubois's regulars. Let's have a look.'

The newsagent glared at them from inside his kiosk. 'We're not a library,' he said grumpily in French.

'We better pay for this one.' Olivia handed over the correct money. 'We'll take it to the café.'

When they were seated, Olivia looked at the caption. 'He's not Monsieur Lambert according to this. He's Monsieur Leroux. Are you sure it's the same man?'

'Absolutely sure. He has an odd-shaped ear - it folds over at the top. There can't be many men who look exactly like that.'

'He must use an alias at Madame Dubois's then.'

'Who is he?'

'The Minister for Justice,' Olivia said. 'Impressive. Madame Dubois provides services for France's elite. She'll be up for a Legion of Honour next.

'No wonder he uses an alias, but you'd think he'd have work to do on Wednesdays at 3 pm.'

'Perhaps the Ministry of Justice is like school - they're all allowed to do sports on Wednesday afternoons,' Olivia said.

Nancy had excused herself from the café as soon as she'd finished eating. 'If you don't mind, I'd prefer to do something more cultural this afternoon,' she had said to Olivia. 'You can go shoe shopping while I head to the Louvre.'

Now she was standing in the foyer of the Louvre studying the visitor's guide. She hadn't appreciated how large the museum was until she saw the layout printed on the back. She'd promised to meet Olivia outside in an hour's time but it was going to take a lot longer than that to do it justice. She decided to concentrate on the most famous exhibits and come back another day to look at the rest.

The Mona Lisa would be a good place to start. She worked out the most efficient route to get to it: up a large stone staircase, then turn right at the top. That brought her out into a long gallery full of enormous oil paintings as well as lots of people. She checked the map again. She needed to turn right at the far end of the gallery but it wasn't going to be easy getting through the crowd. She'd try an alternative route.

She walked into a smaller gallery which was much quieter. As she set off towards the far end, she noticed a man sitting on a bench, entranced by a large landscape. He looked just like Hans. But Hans didn't like art. He'd said that in the café last week when she'd floated the idea of them going to a gallery together for a change.

A woman walked in from the opposite end of the gallery and sat close to the man - so close that if they weren't close friends already, they soon would be. She was smartly dressed with dark hair in a short pixie cut and a distinctive white streak in her fringe. Nancy couldn't decide if it was dyed or natural.

The man turned his head, scanning the room. There was no doubt about it - it was definitely Hans. Nancy quickly turned away so he wouldn't see her face. When she risked turning back, Hans was whispering something in the woman's ear. Nancy felt a pang of jealousy. *You aren't going out with him. He can see other people. You've assumed he's single, but he's never actually said that.* Or perhaps it wasn't jealousy but annoyance that he'd lied to her about not liking art galleries.

No point shilly-shallying, Nancy. Get him to introduce you to her. She marched up to them. The woman got up immediately and left the gallery without even acknowledging Nancy's presence. How bloody rude!

'What a lovely surprise,' Hans said, but his expression said otherwise.

'I thought you didn't like art galleries.'

'I had to meet someone. She suggested here.'

'Who is she?'

'Someone I know from Berlin. It's for work.'

Nancy didn't believe that for a minute. 'Working on a Saturday? That's a bit much, isn't it? She's left her newspaper behind.' Nancy nodded to the folded-up newspaper that was lying next to Hans's thigh, right where the woman had been sitting. It was the same one that Olivia had purchased earlier with Monsieur Lambert on the front.

He grabbed the newspaper and hastily shoved it into his coat pocket. 'She thought I would be interested in one of the articles. Shall we look around the rest of the gallery together while we're both here?' he asked, getting up.

Nancy was still annoyed with him. 'No, I'd prefer to look round alone, thanks.'

He nodded. 'See you after work on Tuesday?'

'I guess so,' she said, walking away.

Olivia was standing outside the main entrance to the Louvre when Nancy emerged.

'Have you been waiting long?' Nancy asked.

'I only just got here,' Olivia said. 'Mission accomplished,' she added, proudly holding up her haul of shopping bags.

Nancy guessed there were at least three shoe boxes in there.

Olivia must have read her mind. 'There was a sale on. They were bargains. How was your cultural interlude?'

'Even more interesting than I expected.'

'Why?'

'I bumped into Hans.'

'That's nice.' Olivia looked delighted.

'And a woman.'

Olivia's face fell. 'What woman?'

Nancy filled her in on what had happened.

'He's not taken Christa anywhere since he started meeting you for English lessons,' Olivia said. 'I thought you were in pole position to be his new love interest. Do you think this woman's a girlfriend?'

'She might be an old flame. Or it could have been a first date, though she knew him well enough to sit right next to him. Whatever she is, he wasn't happy to see me. Weird that she just walked off, though. If they were an item, wouldn't she have stuck around to find out who I was? I know I would. And why bring a newspaper?'

'He might have been telling the truth about her being a work colleague. You'll have to see what you can find out at your next English lesson.'

14

Nancy had had plenty of time over the weekend to work out the best way to subtly quiz Hans about the mysterious woman in the Louvre. She was ready with her plan of action when Hans met her outside the shop on Tuesday afternoon.

'Shall we cover office vocabulary today?' Nancy suggested as she walked with Hans towards the cafe in the park.

'I'm not sure how useful that would be,' he said. Was she imagining it, or did he look worried? Perhaps he'd guessed what she was really interested in discussing.

'Seeing your work colleague in the Louvre at the weekend made me realise that you know exactly what I get up to in the bookshop but you never talk to me about what you do at work,' she said.

'That's because my job is not very interesting,' he assured her. 'It involves creating lots of paperwork that gets sent to the head office in Berlin.'

'What sort of paperwork?'

Hans shrugged. 'Filling out forms. Writing reports. That sort of thing.'

'Export forms?'

'Yes, exactly that.'

'And what sort of things do you write reports on?'

'Oh, um, things going on in Paris.'

'Why would your headquarters in Berlin be interested in that?'

'It helps them to decide what they need to export in future.'

Nancy nodded. It sounded reasonable. But she couldn't care less about the paperwork really. Time to cut to the chase. 'Does your work colleague do that too?'

'Which colleague?'

'The one you met in the Louvre on Saturday. Does she visit Paris often? Or does she work in the Paris office with you all the time?'

'She works in Berlin. She visits here occasionally.'

'It's a shame your employers expect her to work on a Saturday.'

'Lots of Germans work on Saturdays. You work most Saturdays,' he pointed out.

'Yes, but you expect that with shop work. I wouldn't like to have to do that in an office job. Why couldn't she talk to you in the office?'

'It was something confidential.'

'That sounds intriguing?'

'Not really. Shall we walk the opposite way around the lake today?'

'Good idea,' she said. But she wasn't going to let him change the subject that easily. 'When will she be visiting again?'

'Not for several weeks, I think.'

'And does that bother you?'

'Why would it bother me?'

'It looked like you enjoyed your business meetings with her.'

Hans chuckled. 'Are you trawling?'

'Trawling?' Nancy was baffled.

'Yes, trying to find out information in an indirect way?'

So much for being subtle, Nancy! 'You mean fishing.'

'Sorry. Are you fishing?'

'Why would I be fishing?' she said innocently.

'I don't know. But if you were fishing for information on my colleague, I have known her for several years, and we are just friends, not lovers.'

'I wasn't fishing, but that's nice that you're friends.'

'Friendship is very important to me.'

15

It was another quiet day in the bookshop.

'Shall I put the kettle on?' Nancy asked Philip as he lugged another box of new titles out of the office.

'Good idea,' he said, dropping the box by the bookshelf near the window.

Nancy headed into the office. The kettle had just started to whistle when she heard an even more piercing sound coming from inside the shop. It must be some sort of alarm. Was someone breaking into the till? She turned off the hob and started to head back to the shop floor when the office door burst open and Philip ran in.

'Watch the shop!' he shouted as he snatched open the door marked Privé and ran up the stairs to Madame Dubois's private apartments.

What the hell was going on? Nancy was torn between following him and heading back into the shop. She supposed she should do as she was told, but this would be the perfect opportunity to find out what was going on upstairs. She hadn't heard the tinkle of the bell on the shop door since the arrival of Madame Dubois's latest client, so there shouldn't be any customers around. She went inside to check. No. Not a soul. She looked at her watch. It would be lunchtime in fifteen minutes. It wouldn't hurt to shut a bit earlier. It was hardly likely to cost them a sale.

She dropped the lock on the front door and turned the closed sign over, then dashed upstairs to make sure there was no one on floors one or two. They were both empty, but she could hear some muffled shouting and grunting from Madame Dubois's private apartments.

She ran back downstairs. As she opened the door to the back room, Philip ran from Mme Dubois's apartments and picked up the phone.

'Ambulance please,' he said in French, 'It's an emergency. Yes. Yes. Heart problem, I think. Yes. Dubois's books, on the corner of Rue de la Cour and Rue Saint Aubin. Come in via the shop door. Thank you.'

He put the phone down.

'But I've locked the shop door,' Nancy said.

'Well, unlock it,' Philip snapped. 'Monsieur Ferrier has had a heart attack. The ambulance will be here in five minutes. Stand outside and wait for them.'

He ran back upstairs before she could ask any questions.

Nancy didn't argue. By the time she'd unlocked the door and gone out onto the top step, she could hear the distinctive, almost musical sound of an emergency siren.

'We had some excitement at work today,' Nancy said to Olivia when she arrived home. 'I finally got to see inside Madame Dubois's flat'

Nancy had Olivia's complete attention. 'How?'

Nancy explained about poor Monsieur Ferrier. 'I followed the ambulance men upstairs, and there he was, spark out in the floor of the living room.'

'Was he alright?'

'He looked grey, but he was still breathing when they carried him out. And Madame Dubois phoned the hospital this afternoon and they said he was on the mend.'

'Was he fully clothed?'

'Yes.'

'So much for your theory then.'

'But his shirt buttons were done up oddly.'

Olivia looked thoughtful. 'Madame Dubois or Philip could have tried to resuscitate him? You're meant to open the shirt so you can find the right place to push down on the rib cage.'

'But why do his shirt up again? And then there were the moans and groans I heard on the upper floor of the shop. Her living room is nowhere near that part.'

'They must have moved him before the ambulance arrived. No other clues?'

'No. It's a very tastefully decorated Parisian flat, like something you'd see in an interior design magazine.'

'That doesn't tell us anything. Her well-to-do clients are unlikely to want to go somewhere seedy. How much more of the apartment is there?'

'I couldn't tell. All I could see were the living room and a glimpse of a small kitchen. There must be at least one bedroom beyond that.'

'How are you going to find out?'

'I have no idea.'

'Could you sneak up there while she's out?'

Nancy had already considered that. 'What if Philip catches me or Madame Dubois comes back early - what would be my excuse for being there? I need this job. I can't join Patty on the yacht otherwise.'

'We'll have to let our subconsciouses work on the problem. Today hasn't ruled out your theory but it hasn't proved it either.'

16

As she walked into her flat after Hans' latest English lesson, Nancy was hit by the smell of something delicious cooking in the kitchen. Olivia was stirring a large saucepan on the hob.

'You're home!' Nancy said. She'd missed having Olivia around the place. The Easter weekend had dragged without her.

'We got back at lunchtime. I said we would. The traffic wasn't too bad, and Pierre was an excellent driver.'

'Glad he's good at something,' Nancy said as she hung up her coat. 'How was the chateau?'

'Very chateau-like. It has several cute turrets, like something out of a fairytale.'

'Still hoping Pierre will get to inherit it?'

'I don't see why he shouldn't. His parents seem very nice. They were very welcoming to both of us.'

'No sharp intakes of breath at any dresses you wore that were more than two months old?'

'Very funny! Do you want your dinner on a plate or thrown at you?'

Nancy laughed. 'It looks too good to throw. What is it?' she asked, peering over Olivia's shoulder.

'Spaghetti bolognese. It's ready now. Shall I dish up?'

'Yes, please. I like paydays. I'd forgotten what meat smells like.'

'We'll be back on bread and cheese by Friday,' Olivia assured her.

Nancy laid the table while Olivia filled two plates with large portions of pasta and sauce.

'Wine with your meal, madame?' Olivia asked, taking a bottle of white out of the fridge.

'It's Tuesday. What's got into you?'

'Who says we can't have wine on a Tuesday?'

'No one, but I've got work in the morning.'

'You managed to work with the mother of all hangovers the other week, so I'm sure one glass of Sancerre won't negatively impact your ability to sell books tomorrow.'

Nancy studied the very ornate label. 'Is this from Pierre's family's vineyard?'

'Yes. His father sent me home with a whole case of it.' Olivia looked delighted.

'It looks expensive.'

'It is. But I'm hoping he'll give me more next time I visit, so there's no point in storing it away for years.' Olivia expertly removed the cork and poured a couple of glasses. 'Cheers!'

'Cheers!' Nancy clinked her glass against Olivia's.

'What did I miss while I was away?' Olivia asked as she sat down to eat.

'Nothing! It rained most of the weekend. I tidied the flat, wrote a couple of letters home, read a book, and went to the cinema to see *Casablanca,* thinking it would have French subtitles so I could still listen to the soundtrack, but it turned out to be dubbed. It was a good job I remembered the plot. Then I went back to The Louvre.'

'Any sign of Hans there this time?'

'No. I've neither seen nor heard anything from him or Dieter all weekend.'

'Interesting. I thought he might pay you a call. I bumped into him on Friday and made a point of telling him I was going away for a few days.'

'You've got that matchmaking look on your face again. I've told you we're just friends.'

'Who spend an hour together after work at least four times a week.'

'And no time together at weekends even though we're neighbours. You always conveniently forget about that, I notice.'

'I think we should throw a party,' Olivia said.

'Why did talking about Hans prompt you to suggest that?'

'No reason.' Olivia had her best innocent look on her face now. 'I enjoy going to other people's parties. I think it's time I returned the favour, and now there are two of us here to share the organising, it seems like a good time to do it.'

Even if there was an element of matchmaking involved, Nancy was desperate for some more company. 'I'm up for it. When were you thinking?'

'Next Saturday? Then we've got Sunday to recover.'

'Are you planning a boozy do a la Christa and Ingrid?'

'No, we can't afford that. Just some nibbles and a few bottles of cheap plonk - I'm locking the Sancerre away. People usually bring a bottle. We're unlikely to run out.'

'We need to make it more enticing than that. Otherwise, no one will come. Shall we have a theme?'

'Good idea. How about Kings and Queens?' Olivia suggested.

'The costumes might be tricky. We don't want it to look naff.'

'Ok then.' Olivia looked excited. 'Greeks and Romans. All you need is a sheet and a belt, and it's toga time.'

'Isn't that a bit naff as well?'

'Probably, but it requires minimal effort. And you'll get to find out if Hans has attractive calves, too. It's impossible to tell with those baggy suits he wears.'

Nancy hadn't thought about the shape of Hans' calves, though she had wondered about other parts of him. 'We're inviting Hans, are we?'

'It would be rude not to. "We like you, but when it comes to partying, you can stay downstairs and listen to the rest of us getting steadily drunker." Not very friendly, is it?'

'Who else are we going to ask?'

'Pierre, Dieter, Christa, Ingrid, their Californian neighbours - they're always a good laugh. What about Philip?'

'Yes, he might be fun.'

'Carol?'

Nancy hadn't got Carol down as a party animal. 'I guess if I slipped the invite into whatever book she's currently engrossed in, she might read it.'

'There are a few more people at work I'd like you to meet. I'll include them. It should be an excellent do if they all come.'

'A toga party?' Hans said when Nancy gave him his invitation the following day.

'Yes, they're the dress things that ancient Romans used to wear.'

'I understand. It's the same word in German.'

'Is it? I suppose that makes sense. It doesn't have to be a real toga. A sheet and a belt will do.'

'It could be fun,' Hans said.

Nancy was pleasantly surprised. She'd half expected him to turn the offer down as he didn't seem to be interested in socialising outside of their English lessons. 'You'll come then?'

'It will be worth the journey, I'm sure,' he grinned. 'Will there be music?'

'Whatever's on the radio, unless Olivia decides to sing. I won't be encouraging her to do that unless everyone is completely drunk. It's not a pleasant experience for anyone.'

'You can borrow my record player. It sounds like it might be less painful.'

'Really? That would be lovely. I had to leave mine at home. What records have you got that we can dance to?'

'The Beatles, Bill Hailey. A whole mix of things.'

So, he had good taste in music as well. *Don't think about him as potential boyfriend material again - you know you said you weren't going to get involved*! 'You're an angel,' she said.

'I don't know about that,' he said. 'Who else is invited?'

She reeled off the list of names. 'Everyone's said yes so far, apart from Philip. He's off to the South of France with a friend for the weekend.'

'I shall look forward to it,' Hans said, looking like he meant it.

17

The day of the party soon came around. Olivia was fretting about her cheese and pineapple sticks. 'They won't stay upright. It looks such a mess.'

'We should've got a grapefruit to stick them into,' Nancy said.

'It's too late now. Everyone will start arriving soon.' Olivia added the dish to the array of food and drink on the table. 'We need to move that sofa. There's no room for anyone to dance.'

'Relax! Hans will be here any minute. I'm sure he'll help.'

'Pierre is conspicuous by his absence. He promised he'd arrive early, too.'

Nancy was about to suggest that Olivia calmed her nerves with a glass of wine when there was a knock at the door.

'Looks like one of them is here,' Nancy said, opening the apartment door. 'Hi, Hans.'

'I bring music,' he said, holding a Dansette record player with what looked like a bag of records hanging off his arm. 'Where do you want it?'

'She could tell you,' Olivia winked at him.

It never ceased to amaze Nancy how the presence of an attractive man instantly transformed Olivia into an outrageous flirt.

Hans looked bemused. Nancy hoped he didn't ask her to explain at their next lesson.

'In the corner over there will be fine,' she said. 'There's a power socket next to the table.'

'And when you've done that, move the sofa back against the wall.' Olivia said. 'I need to check we have toilet roll.'

'Anything else, madame?' Hans asked.

Olivia missed the subtext as she headed into the bathroom

Nancy smiled at Hans. 'I'm sorry. She gets very bossy when she's stressed.'

'So I see,' he said. 'Your toga suits you.'

'You're not looking too bad yourself,' she grinned. 'Though I'm not sure pale pink is your colour.'

'Unfortunately, only pink sheets came with the flat.'

'We've got a spare white one if you want to get changed?' *Bad idea, Nancy, but you've offered now!*

Hans didn't seem worried by the suggestion. 'If you think it would be better.'

'It would. That pink is doing nothing for your skin tone. Come with me.'

Hans followed Nancy into Olivia's room. She rifled through the ottoman at the end of the bed. 'Here we are,' she said, shaking out a large, flat white sheet.

Hans took off his belt. The pink sheet fell to the floor, leaving him standing in nothing but tight-fitting swim shorts. It was a lot to take in.

He looked embarrassed and started picking up his sheet. 'I'm sorry. That wasn't meant to happen.'

She kept her gaze above his waist level. His abs were impressive, but something else had caught her eye.

'What's that scar?' Nancy resisted the temptation to touch the four-inch-long red mark near his right shoulder.

'It was an accident. It will fade eventually,' he said.

It looked fairly recent. 'I bet that hurt.'

He shrugged. 'It's ok now.'

He looked vulnerable standing there. She felt the urge to hug him and a lot more besides.

'Nancy! What the hell are you doing?' The sound of her father's outraged shout ruined the moment. For a second, she thought she'd imagined him, but no, he was actually standing there in Olivia's doorway.

Nancy was horrified. 'Dad?! What are you doing here?'

'Why are you half naked?' her father asked, storming into the room. 'And why isn't this man wearing any clothes? What is this? An orgy?'

'We're about to have a toga party,' Nancy said.

'Calm down, George,' Nancy's mother said, following her husband into the bedroom. 'Think of your blood pressure.'

She turned to Nancy. 'Hello, darling. You weren't expecting us, then?'

'No, it's a complete surprise. Why have you come all this way?' Nancy was trying desperately to think of a way to get rid of them quickly. After seeing more of Hans than either of them intended, her resolve to remain friends had faded. Her parents arriving now couldn't be worse timing.

'We've missed you so much,' her mother continued. 'I wrote to say I'd persuaded your father that a spring break in Paris would be lovely and an ideal excuse to make sure you were alright. I've booked a table for the three of us at the bistro on the corner.'

A meal out with them. Nancy couldn't think of anything worse at this precise moment. 'I never got your letter,' she said.

Nancy's mother looked at her pleadingly. 'I'm sorry if we've spoilt your plans, but I'm sure your friends will still be having a lovely party after we've eaten.'

Nancy didn't know what to say. She turned to Hans, who by now had wrapped himself up in the white sheet.

'Your friend can come too.' Nancy's mother said, holding her hand out to Hans.

'Thank you, Mrs Smith,' he smiled, shaking it.

'Are you German?' Nancy's father growled.

'Yes, he is,' Nancy snapped. 'It's very cosmopolitan here.'

Nancy's father stormed out of the room.

Hans looked uncomfortable. 'It's a kind offer, Mrs Smith, but I think it would be best if I didn't join you.'

Nancy had reluctantly agreed to leave the party to join her parents for their evening meal and swapped her toga for a more conventional dress. The atmosphere at their table was tense.

Nancy's father was glaring at the menu. 'I don't want anything with garlic in it.'

The waiter was unimpressed. 'I think you will find that it adds interest and flavour to the dishes, monsieur.'

'I don't care. I don't want it. Awful stuff. And don't you get ordering it either, Daphne. I don't want to breathe in your garlic fumes all night.'

Nancy glanced at the waiter, hoping her expression looked suitably apologetic. 'Stick to the steak, Dad. With pommes frites.'

'What on earth are those?' he snapped.

'Chips,' she said.

Her father huffed.

The waiter took that as confirmation of his order. 'And you, madame?' he said, turning to Nancy's mother.

'Moules marinières s'il vous plait,' she said.

Nancy was relieved that at least one of her parents was trying to avoid a diplomatic incident. The waiter nodded approvingly. 'Avec de l'ail?'

'Avec beaucoup de l'ail,' Nancy's mother said.

The waiter smiled. Nancy suppressed a grin at her mother's request for lots of garlic. She was glad she wouldn't be anywhere near her parents' hotel later.

When the waiter left, her mother reached across the table and took her husband's hand. 'You had something you wanted to say to Nancy, didn't you, darling.'

Nancy's father scowled back at his wife. She raised her eyebrows.

'Yes, I suppose I did,' he said. 'I may have been a bit harsh when I banned you from coming here. Not that it made any difference.'

Nancy sat silently, waiting to see what was coming next.

'And?' her mother prompted him.

'And I understand why you left. I want to offer you a chance to become a management trainee.'

He didn't look like that's what he wanted at all.

'And what's prompted that?' Nancy asked. 'Has Eddie gone to the States?'

Her father shifted uncomfortably in his chair. 'He'll be going in a few weeks.'

Nancy wasn't impressed. 'I see. Your son has confirmed he has no interest in taking over the family business, so in the absence of any other male offspring, you're grudgingly offering me the opportunity instead?'

'I'm doing no such thing. I'm offering you a trainee job.'

'No, George,' her mother said. 'You are absolutely offering Nancy the opportunity to become your successor.'

Nancy walked back up the stairs to the apartment. The whole building sounded quiet, but it was only just after 10 pm. Surely the party hadn't ended already. She let herself into the flat. Olivia was washing up at the sink, but there was no sign of anyone else.

'Did we have a good party?' Nancy asked, grabbing a tea towel and starting to dry the glasses.

'Yes, we did, but we missed you. Hans left shortly after you did. He said he'd pick up his record player tomorrow. Everyone else gave up about half an hour ago when the wine ran out. They were talking about going on to a club, but I said I'd wait for you here. How was your meal?'

'I'm sure it would have tasted a lot better if I didn't have to put up with Dad looking at me disapprovingly throughout both courses. I've got terrible indigestion now.'

'What awful timing.'

'There is never a good time for my beloved father to turn up anywhere. I should have told them to go, but I couldn't do that to Mum.'

'Were they just here to check up on you?' Olivia asked.

'No. Dad made me an interesting offer.'

Olivia stopped washing up. 'Well?'

'He's offering me the chance to train to be his successor.'

'Wow! That's a turn-up for the books. What did you say?'

'What do you think I said? It's only because Eddie's not interested.'

'You turned him down?'

'Of course I did. You know what he's like. I can either spend the winter battling wind, rain and turbulent seas, or I can sit in the office next to his, on tenterhooks, waiting for him to berate me for whatever error I've allegedly made that day.'

Olivia nodded. 'Given that choice, even I would pick the turbulent seas. Are you seeing your folks again?'

'They've gone back to their hotel. Mum asked me to come on a boat trip with them tomorrow, but I said I had to work.'

'On a Sunday?'

'They didn't question it. They're flying back home in the afternoon. I'll feel much more relaxed once they've left French airspace.'

18

Pierre had taken Olivia for a picnic lunch, leaving Nancy alone in the flat, mulling over last night's events. She didn't waste much time thinking about her father's offer - she was confident turning him down was the right decision.

Instead, she focused on Hans. She was attracted to him. She'd even dreamt about him last night. They were on Patty's yacht, just the two of them sailing off into the sunset and doing plenty of other things as well. Nancy felt a warm glow at the memory.

But did he feel the same way about her? He'd left the party just after she had. Surely, that was a positive sign? *Or he might have been feeling unwell or any number of other reasons that had nothing to do with missing you.* Thank you, inner voice, for putting the dampers on that theory.

She noticed his record player on the table in the corner. *Why not take it back to him?*

No time like the present. She unplugged the player, grabbed his bag of records, and headed downstairs to the flat below.

Dieter answered the door.

'Is Hans in?' she asked.

Dieter grinned. 'Good timing. He's cooking lunch for me and Ingrid.' He took the record player out of her arms. 'Hey, Hans. Your English teacher is here.'

Nancy spotted Hans bending down, looking in the oven.

He turned around and smiled. 'Hello, Nancy.'

'I didn't realise you'd be busy. I brought your records back.'

'Thanks. Would you like to stay for some food? I am cooking beef bourguignon.'

She better not mention that she'd eaten the same dish last night. 'That would be lovely. Are you sure?'

'There is a lot,' he said. 'It will be ready in five minutes, I think. Please sit down at the table.'

Dieter got another knife and fork and put them down in front of Nancy.

Ingrid smiled. 'It's nice that you're here to even up the numbers.' She raised her eyebrows at Nancy. Was she matchmaking now? Hopefully, Olivia and Ingrid wouldn't join forces. If she was as unsubtle as Olivia, between them, they could ruin whatever chance Nancy had with Hans.

Nancy changed the subject. 'I didn't realise you cooked, Hans.'

'Dieter doesn't, so I have to. Not that I mind.'

'And I enjoy being cooked for,' Ingrid said. 'Which means you'll need to learn if you want us to have a future together, Dieter.'

Dieter looked worried. 'Hans will have to give me lessons.'

Hans put the casserole in the middle of the table, followed by a dish of mashed potatoes. 'Help yourselves,' he said, sitting next to Nancy.

Ingrid distributed the food. Nancy tried a mouthful of the stew. It was even tastier than last night's bistro offering. *Another tick in the box for Hans.* 'It's delicious,' she said.

They chatted about their weekends. Nancy noticed how the banter between Dieter and Hans was similar to the way she and Olivia spoke to one another. She was glad he had a close friend. It must mean the world to him with no family to turn to.

The topic of conversation turned to last night's party. 'We had a great time. Why did you leave so early?' Ingrid asked Hans.

'I wasn't in a party mood after Nancy left.' Hans glanced at Nancy.

'I'm sorry I had to go. And I'm sorry how my father behaved,' she said.

'It's not your fault. Though it could be awkward in future.'

What did he mean by that? *Stop overanalysing everything and just enjoy being here.*

'I think we should leave now,' Ingrid said to Dieter when everyone had finished eating.

'Should we? Why?' He flinched as Ingrid kicked him under the table. 'OK. We're going.'

'Enjoy the rest of your day,' Ingrid said as they headed out the door. 'I'll make sure Dieter isn't back until late tonight.'

As Nancy had suspected, Ingrid was as subtle as Olivia when it came to fixing people up.

'I'll help you clear away,' Nancy said to Hans once they were alone.

'No, it's not necessary. You're my guest.'

'I don't mind.'

'I do. Shall I put some music on? Perhaps we can dance like we should've done last night?'

That sounded very promising. 'I'd like that. I've been wondering how good a dancer you are.'

He smiled. 'I expect you're a much better dancer than me. What would you like to dance to?'

'Surprise me,' she said, thinking his song choice should give her a clue how he felt.

He started flicking through his record collection. 'Before I forget, I have to return to Berlin tomorrow.'

'Oh.' What did he mean by return? Surely not forever?

He must have noticed her expression. 'Only for a few days,' he added. 'I have to sort something out with my manager. But it means we'll have to cancel next week's English lessons.'

'Of course.' Nancy did a lousy job of hiding her disappointment.

'I only found out yesterday. I was planning to tell you last night. I'll be back as soon as I can,' he reassured her.

'Good,' she said.

He started putting a record on the player. 'Ready?' he asked.

'As I'll ever be,' she smiled.

He looked puzzled.

'It means yes.'

'Excellent,' he said, pulling back the lever that made the arm of the player move across to the disc.

But before the needle touched the vinyl, there was a loud banging on the door. 'Herr Schmidt, Herr Schmidt,' a voice called out. It sounded like Madame Morceau.

Hans looked disappointed. He put the record player arm back on its rest and opened the flat door.

'Thank God you are in.' Madame Morceau let out a sigh. 'There is water pouring down the wall of the flat below. Madame Chastain is most distressed.'

'Pierre gave me some hot chocolate,' Olivia said when she returned home that evening.

'That's an unusual present.' Nancy looked at the jar.

'Yes, I'm not sure what it says about our relationship. Either it's a subtle way of telling me I'm not hot enough, or we've got to the point where he'll be buying me slippers and a bed jacket next. Which is a shame because he seems to have skipped the gold and diamonds stage. I was looking forward to that. We may as well drink it, though.'

'Hmm,' Nancy said.

'You don't have to if you don't want to.'

'It's not that. I was just thinking it was the only thing that was going to warm me up today.'

'You're going to have to elaborate on that one. I haven't got a clue what you're talking about.'

Nancy brought Olivia up to speed about the afternoon's events.

'So Madame Chastain's plumbing got in the way of a romantic afternoon?' Olivia said.

'It was Hans' plumbing, actually. We eventually established the water running down her wall was coming from a leaky cold water pipe under his bath. It's all turned off now, and the plumber's coming to fix it tomorrow. But by the time we reached that point, the moment had gone. He needed to pack for his Berlin trip. He'll have left France now.'

19

Nancy was home early. She'd gone to the café in the Bois de Boulogne without Hans yesterday, but it felt odd sitting at their usual table on her own, so this afternoon, she'd headed straight for the flat.

When she arrived at their apartment building, she checked their postbox. There were two envelopes for Olivia and just one letter for her. It was postmarked Portsmouth and looked like Patty's writing, which sprawled across the envelope, giving the impression that she'd written it in a hurry. Hopefully, all was still going well with Patty's round-the-world sailing plans. Nancy put Olivia's letters in her bag and ripped open Patty's so she could read it as she climbed the stairs:

Dear Nancy

Hope you're having an amazing time in Paris. It's still all systems go here on the good ship Boadicea. (Did I tell you that's what we've decided to call her now? We can't have a bunch of women setting a world record in a vessel called King Henry VIII!!!)

Nancy grinned at the new name. Good job she wasn't superstitious - she could picture some of the old sailors in the harbour at Dashford sucking disapprovingly on their pipes at the idea of renaming a boat. Patty, of course, had already thought of that:

Don't worry! I threw a shilling in the sea so Neptune won't plague us with bad luck. (Not sure shillings are real silver now, but I can't see how an old sea god is going to test that underwater.)

Anyway, slight problem: the refit was more expensive than I expected. So sorry, but we're £300 short, which means I need every crew member to stump up an extra £30. Trust that won't be a problem.

Much love,

P xx

Bugger! Nancy did a quick calculation in her head. £30 was over three weeks' wages. How was she going to find that between now and June?

She reached the top of the stairs and let herself into their apartment. She needed to find the notebook that held all her savings plans.

Half an hour later, Nancy was referring to her notes and scribbling sums on scrap paper. No matter what she did, she couldn't work out how to save another £30. £10 maybe, but certainly not £30. She could write to her mother to see if she could give her a loan, but if her father intercepted it, he would find a way to stop her from going on the trip. He was even more annoyed with her after seeing her with Hans at the party.

A knock at the door interrupted her train of thought. Olivia was meant to be seeing Pierre this evening. They must have had yet another row. She sighed and got up. 'Have you forgotten your keys?' she said as she opened the door.

'No, I never had any.' Hans was smiling back at her. Her heart skipped a beat. She'd missed that smile even though he'd only been gone for two days.

'Sorry, I thought you were Olivia.' She welcomed him in.

'I hope I'm not too much of a disappointment.'

'Of course not. It's a lovely surprise. You said you weren't going to be back until Friday.'

'I got my work done early.'

'Is your manager happy with you again?'

'It would seem so, yes.'

She noticed he was dressed more casually than usual. 'New jumper?'

'Sweater?' Hans said.

'No - it's a jumper. "Sweater" sounds very American. I would call that a navy blue polo-necked jumper.'

Hans nodded. 'I'll remember that. Do you like it?'

'Yes, it suits you.' It really did. The blue enhanced his eyes, and it fitted well, reminding her of the decent physique he had underneath. Nancy looked away quickly before he realised she was mentally undressing him.

'Have you taken up accountancy?' he asked, looking at the sheets of paper covered in numbers that were spread out on the dining table.'

'No, though I will have to take up a new profession to afford everything.'

Hans looked puzzled.

'I need an extra 400 francs for my sailing trip,' she explained.

'I thought you said you'd got it all planned out.'

'I had, but the price has gone up. Our captain has gone overboard on the refit.'

Hans looked shocked. 'She's fallen in the sea?'

Nancy smiled. 'No, she's fine. It means she spent more than she intended.'

'Oh. I had not heard that phrase before. So what are you going to do?'

'Stop eating?'

'I can help with that a little. I can save you some money on food this evening,' he said with a grin. 'Would you like to join me for a meal?'

'At yours?'

'No. A meal in a restaurant cooked by a proper chef this time. One who comes highly recommended. I will pay. I'm sure there is a better way to say that.'

'My treat?'

'Yes, that's it. My treat. It's my birthday, so you would be doing me a kindness by not letting me eat alone.'

'Happy Birthday! I'm sorry I haven't got you a present.'

'As I didn't tell you it was my birthday, I don't think you need to apologise,' he said. 'The pleasure of your company will more than make up for it.'

'You're a gentleman, Hans,' she smiled.

'I try hard to be.'

'The restaurant is only a few minutes' away,' Hans said as they set off up the street. 'It's called Les Deux Chat Noir.'

After a few turns, he pointed to an ornate Art Nouveau clock on the wall opposite with two black cats painted on the dial. 'We have arrived,' he said, crossing the road and holding the door open for her.

The maitre d' recognised him straightway. 'Bonjour, Monsieur Schmidt,' he nodded. 'One moment.' He headed towards the back of the restaurant.

'You've been here before then?' Nancy asked, suspecting that this was one of the venues where he used to woo Christa. Had he brought the woman with the white hair streak here, too?

'I've eaten here a few times. It was good, but there is a new chef now, one who is even better than the previous one.'

The maitre d' returned. 'Your usual table is ready, monsieur,' he said, ushering the pair of them to a cosy corner at the back of the restaurant. 'I trust this is fine?'

'Yes, excellent, thank you,' Hans said.

The maitre d' pulled out Nancy's chair and settled her at the table, handing her the thick linen napkin.

'I will be back to take your order shortly,' the maitre d' said, bowing slightly, as another waiter placed the menus and the wine list on the table.

'This is posh,' Nancy said, stroking the expensive leather on the menu.

'Posh? Is that bad?' he asked, sounding worried.

'No. It means expensive, something that is good quality.'

'You deserve something posh,' he laughed. 'I suspect you are used to posh restaurants at home.'

Nancy laughed. She loved how he tried out new words as soon as he learnt them. 'Sadly not. My father considers eating out to be a major extravagance.'

'I thought you said he owned a factory.'

'He does, and it earns him a lot of money, but he doesn't like to spend it, not on his family anyway.'

'What does he spend it on?'

'Houses mostly. To rent out to people to make even more money.'

'That seems to be what capitalism is about. Is he a good landlord?'

'I suspect not, given how mean he is with us.'

She was relieved that the waiter picked that moment to return to take their order.

'I have absolutely no idea what to choose,' Nancy said, glancing down the bewildering list of options.

'Shall I choose for you? Is there anything you don't eat?' Hans asked.

'Lamb chops. I've eaten enough of those to last a lifetime.'

'Very well.' He began reeling off a list of dishes in what sounded like perfect French. The waiter complimented him on his choices.

'So what are we having?' Nancy asked as the waiter walked away.

'It will be a surprise. Hopefully, a good one.'

Another waiter appeared with a bottle of red wine. It looked expensive. 'Wine, Madame?'

Madame not mademoiselle. Perhaps the dim lighting made her look older, or was he just being respectful?

'Yes, please.'

She noticed how the candle flame made Hans' eyes sparkle more than usual. At least, she assumed it was the candle.

She raised her glass to him. 'Happy Birthday, Hans.'

'That was a wonderful meal. Thank you,' Nancy said as they left the restaurant.

'I'm glad you enjoyed it.'

Nancy shivered when the cool evening air hit her bare arms.

'Are you ok?' Hans asked.

'I should've remembered to bring a coat. It was so mild when we set out earlier, I forgot it would be cold now.'

'Take mine.' He took off his jacket and put it around her.

'But what about you?'

'I'm fine. I have my new sweater. Sorry, polo-necked jumper.'

'You're a fast learner,' she giggled at him. *Careful, Nancy, that wine was stronger than you thought.*

'Shall we head back home?' Hans asked.

'Tempting as it would be to stay out longer, I guess we should go home as it's a school night.'

'School night?'

She laughed again. 'I never realised how many idioms we use in English until I started teaching you.'

'I am guessing that you are not going to school tonight.' He grinned.

'No, I'm not. I'm not planning to go to school tonight or any other night. It means we're working tomorrow, so we should go to bed early.' She flushed at what she'd just said. Perhaps that wasn't such a bad idea. From the look in his eyes, he appeared to be thinking the same.

She tilted her face up and tentatively brushed her lips against his. He hesitated for a moment, then kissed her back. His lips were soft against hers. As their tongues met, her whole body felt on fire. Kissing Billy hadn't been a patch on this.

'Let's go home,' he murmured as he pulled away.

She smiled at him as he took her hand and led her through the maze of streets. She held his jacket tightly around her shoulders and imagined having the rest of him wrapped around her very soon.

It seemed to take forever to arrive at his apartment door. By the time they got there, Hans looked on edge. 'I'll see you to your flat.'

'We'd be better off at yours,' she said. 'Olivia's home tonight, and your bed's bigger than mine.'

He shook his head and avoided eye contact. 'Dieter will be home soon, too. Perhaps this is a good thing.' He started walking up the stairs.

'And what's that meant to mean?' she asked as she followed him.

'I don't want to take advantage of you.'

'I'm not that innocent if that's what you're worried about.'

They were outside the door to her flat now. She leaned in to kiss him, but he backed away.

'You're an amazing woman. But I won't make you happy.'

'I don't understand. You already make me happy. I'd appreciate it if you could make me even happier.'

'We should just be friends. I shouldn't have kissed you. I'm so sorry.' He turned to walk away.

What the hell was going on? There was no way he didn't mean that kiss. It wasn't as if she'd pinned him down and forced her tongue down his throat. And what about Sunday afternoon? If they hadn't been interrupted, she was sure something would've happened then.

'Your jacket,' she said, holding it out to him.

'Thank you.' He took it from her without looking her in the eye. 'Good night, Nancy.'

How dare he just walk away like that! She heard the door to his flat click shut, and the bolt go across. That sounded final. She got her keys out and let herself into her own flat.

Olivia was in her bedroom, putting curlers in her hair. 'Was that Hans' voice I heard? I thought he was away?'

'It was Hans. And I'd rather not talk about it.'

'Why? What's he done?'

'It's more what he hasn't done.'

'You can't leave it like that. Dish the dirt, Nancy.'

'We kissed.'

'At last. And?'

'And nothing. He apologised and dumped me on our doorstep.'

'Dumped?'

'In every sense of the word. I'm going to bed. Alone.'

20

The following day, Nancy was washing up the dirty dishes in the bookshop's back room before they closed up for the night. Philip walked in, carrying an empty teacup.

'You missed this one,' he said, putting it in the washing-up bowl. 'Almost home time. Your boyfriend's waiting in the café opposite already.'

'What boyfriend?' Nancy started to dry one of the freshly washed saucers vigorously.

'Hans, of course. How many admirers have you got?'

'He's a friend, not a boyfriend.' The words came out more bitterly than she intended.

'I'm sensing that's not how you want it to be.'

Philip might be able to offer some advice. Nancy had left the flat early that morning to avoid having a detailed post-date analysis session with Olivia, but she regretted that now. She needed someone else as a sounding board for the thoughts that had been whizzing around her head all day.

'If a man kissed you passionately, then apologised and said he only wanted to be friends, what would you think?' she asked.

'I'd think he was a fool for missing out on all this,' he said, striking a classic bodybuilder pose.

Nancy laughed.

'Sorry, it's not funny, is it.'

'Hans wined me and dined me last night. We kissed when we left the restaurant - and I don't just mean a chaste peck on the cheek. He seemed eager to get home, so everything was shaping up for an active night between the sheets, shall we say. And then, as soon as we arrived at his flat, he said we should just be friends.'

Philip took the saucer and tea towel out of Nancy's hands, put them on the draining board and pulled her into a hug. 'It's his loss, not yours. Perhaps he has a terrible venereal disease and didn't want to pass it on?'

'If he has, why did he lead me on?' She eased herself out of Philip's arms - his embrace was comforting, but it made her think of what she had missed out on last night.

'Because you're irresistible.'

'Stop taking the Mickey.'

'I'm not. You're an attractive woman. It sounds like he panicked. You can be intimidating sometimes. What did you talk about on the way home?' Philip asked.

'We walked back in silence, so it wasn't as if I said anything to turn him off. And how am I intimidating?' Nancy didn't think she'd done anything to intimidate Hans. Quite the opposite.

'You know what you want, and you aren't afraid to ask for it. Not all men can cope with that.'

'Are you saying I should play the demure little woman?'

'Good god, no. Be yourself. Were you sober when all this happened?'

'I had a couple of glasses of wine, but I wasn't drunk.'

'He might have been worried you'd regret it when you woke up this morning.'

'Possibly.'

'Are you meant to meet him for an English lesson today?'

'We haven't made any arrangements. He was supposed to be away all week.'

'It's a positive sign that he's here, then.'

'Or he just wants a coffee.'

'And of the hundreds of cafés in Paris, he happens to choose the one opposite where you work right at the time when you're due to leave. I'd say he wants to talk.'

'I'm not sure that I want to talk, though. I'm still angry with him.'

'You don't have to talk to him if you don't want to. Best not to if you're still angry.'

'I guess I've been a bit harsh. My ego's taken a bruising,' Nancy said.

But as she wasn't in the mood for talking to Hans, it was going to be awkward if he was waiting for her in the cafe opposite. She considered sneaking out the back door, but he'd still see her unless she made a very long detour. She'd just have to make a run for it and hope he didn't spot her in time.

Nancy quickly finished the rest of the washing up, grabbed her bag and headed for the shop door. 'Night, Philip.'

'Night, Nancy. Good luck,' he said.

Nancy kept her head down as she exited the shop and turned towards home. Within a few seconds, she heard Hans call out from behind her.

'Nancy! Wait!'

Keep walking! He eventually caught up with her at the traffic lights on the main road.

'You're in a hurry this evening,' he said, slightly out of breath. 'I wondered if we could go for a walk in the Bois like we usually do.'

She decided to be honest. 'Not today, Hans. I'm still upset about last night.' A small gap in the traffic gave her an opportunity to walk away. She looked back at him from the other side of the road. He was staring after her. She waved and walked off, her head held high.

21

The following day was warm and sunny. Too warm and sunny to be stuck indoors.

'How can it be this hot in April?' Nancy said, fanning herself with a leaflet for a local theatre group.

'Summer's arrived early.' Philip opened one of the shop windows in an attempt to let some fresh air inside.

'I'm thirsty. I'll make us some tea.' Nancy headed into the kitchen, which was even more hot and stuffy.

She opened the back door to let in the light breeze. When she turned back to the hob, she suddenly felt something soft rubbing around her ankles. She looked down to see a cute feline face looking up at her. 'Mimi! You made me jump.'

The cat meowed and carried on weaving around Nancy's legs. 'I haven't got anything for you.'

Mimi appeared to understand. She sauntered across the room in the direction of the open door.

Nancy carried on making the drinks, but as she picked up the teapot, she heard the distinctive creak of the door to Madame Dubois's private apartment opening. Strange. Madame Dubois was at the hairdresser's this afternoon. She swung around just in time to see Mimi's fluffy tail disappearing up the stairs. She must have opened the door herself.

'Mimi! Mimi!' Nancy called up the stairs. The cat stared at her from landing, then defiantly carried on up the next flight.

Madame Dubois wasn't going to be happy. For Mimi's safety, Nancy ought to retrieve her. And it was an excellent excuse to check out more of Madame Dubois's flat. She might be able to get to the bottom of what actually went on up there. She headed upstairs.

The living room was as neat and tidy as it had been a few weeks ago when Monsieur Ferrier had had his unfortunate heart attack. But there was no sign of Mimi.

'Mimi! Mimi!' Nancy started making kissing noises as well to see if the cat would respond to them. There was still no sign of her. The door to the kitchen was wide open. She walked in, but the cat wasn't in there either.

Nancy noticed another door ajar on the opposite side of the living room. It led onto a carpeted corridor with several more doors. That's where Mimi must be - there was nowhere else for her to go.

Nancy hesitated. *Don't be a wuss! You wanted some excitement.* It wasn't that risky. Based on previous hairdresser visits, Madame Dubois wouldn't be back for at least another hour.

Nancy headed down the corridor. All the doors were firmly shut except one. Nancy pushed it open.

'There you are, you daft animal!' Mimi was lounging on a leather padded stool, looking like she had no intention of going anywhere. As Nancy approached her, the cat casually lifted her hind leg and carefully started licking between the pads of her rear left paw. Nancy looked around. Unlike the bright light rooms elsewhere in the flat, this one was painted deep red with no windows. Nancy did a double take. The wall colour wasn't the only unusual thing. She took in the chains and ropes hanging on one wall and the handcuffs that were attached to Mimi's stool. A large cage stood in the corner with a selection of whips hanging above it. Nancy stepped outside the room again and worked out where it fitted in the building. It must be close to the second floor of the bookshop. Was this where all the moans and groans had been coming from?

The words "bespoke bindings" floated back into her mind. She chuckled to herself. So that's what this was all about. Obvious really. Billy had said some people got a kick out of being tied up and flogged, but she couldn't understand the appeal personally.

Philip must be in on it. That's why he responded to the alarm when Monsieur Ferrier had the heart attack and why he had a remarkable lack of interest in reading for someone who'd spent nearly three years working in a bookshop. Madame Dubois hadn't employed him for his in-depth knowledge of English literature. She needed someone strong enough to carry a client into the living room if something untoward happened in here, and presumably someone capable of ejecting any unruly clients, too. It all made sense now.

Should she tell Olivia what was going on? She'd think about that later, but right now, the priority had to be evicting Mimi. The cat sensed what Nancy was planning and took evasive action by shooting off the stool and crawling under the bed.

'Come on, Mimi. Play the game.' Nancy lay flat on the floor and looked the cat in the eye. 'You can't stay there. You know Madame Dubois is not your biggest fan.'

Mimi just meowed.

This wasn't going to work. Nancy needed to find something to tempt her out. She went back to the kitchen and looked in the fridge. Surely, there would be some cooked meat in there. But Madame Dubois seemed to survive entirely on white wine. There wasn't even any milk, but there was a small piece of Gruyère at the back of the bottom shelf. Most cats liked cheese, didn't they? *Only one way to find out, Nancy.* She took a knife from the draining board and cut off a sliver. Madame Dubois wouldn't miss that.

She headed back to the dungeon room. As soon as she opened the door, Mimi shot out.

'You infuriating animal,' Nancy said, following her back to the living room. She wafted the piece of cheese in front of her.

Mimi took a step forward and sniffed at it apprehensively. Nancy moved towards the cat's left flank while Mimi considered whether the cheese was edible or not. She dropped the cheese and quickly grabbed the cat with both hands, tucking her under her arm. Mimi meowed in frustration.

'Sorry, Mimi. It's time to go.' But as she set off towards the stairs, she heard voices: Madame Dubois and a male voice she didn't recognise.

In hindsight, the sensible course of action would have been to carry Mimi calmy to the stairs, tell Madame Dubois what had happened, missing out the part about discovering the dungeon, and then leave her to it. But Nancy panicked. She turned around and fled with Mimi into the corridor, pulling the living room door quietly shut after her.

'Now what are we going to do?' she muttered.

Mimi was so bemused by the sudden movement she relaxed in Nancy's arms.

There was no point in going back into the windowless dungeon, as chances were, that was precisely where Madame Dubois and her visitor were heading. Nancy opened the door to one of the rooms that she guessed must face onto the side street. It was a small bedroom, tastefully decorated in a very similar style to the living room. French windows opened onto the side balcony. There was no chance Madame Dubois or her client would come in here, was there? She heard their voices getting closer. It sounded like they were right outside the door now.

If one of them walked in, how was she going to explain why she was standing here cuddling a cat? Nancy peered out at the balcony. It extended across the whole side of the bookshop. If she went out there, there was enough room to stand out of sight of the windows.

She quickly pulled back the net curtain, opened the door and went outside, pulling the curtain across again after herself and clipping the door shut. She'd wait out here for a few minutes until Madame Dubois and her client were busy in the dungeon, then go back inside and retreat to the office downstairs.

Except there was no handle on the outside of the door. Shit! Nancy looked down into the street two floors below. *What are you going to do now, Nancy? You're well and truly stuck.*

Mimi didn't seem too happy about the situation either. She squirmed out of Nancy's arms and leapt onto the top of the ornate ironwork railings that surrounded the balcony, then launched herself across to the next balcony, which belonged to the café where she officially lived.

'That's alright for you, Mimi, but what about me?' Nancy whispered. She considered clambering over the railings and lowering herself down, but she would still be too far off the ground to land safely.

Mimi was miaowing at next door's window. Perhaps someone would let Nancy in, too, if she joined Mimi's on the other balcony. The gap between the two balconies wasn't that big. Nancy clambered onto the ironwork, supporting herself by putting one hand on the wall. She composed herself, ready to jump.

'Nancy! What are you doing?'

She looked down to see Hans standing in the street. Why was he there? He should be importing and exporting things at his office at this time of day. 'You're going to fall,' he said.

'Shh!' She put her fingers to her lips and then pointed at the next balcony. She tried to mime jumping across.

Hans looked horrified. He put his hands up and shook his head. 'Don't move. I'll get help.'

She waved to try to stop him, but he was already heading around the corner, presumably to the bookshop.

Nancy weighed up the jump again. Perhaps Hans was right. It was too far to attempt it in a narrow skirt. If she missed, she'd land on the sweet old lady who had just sat down at the cafe table immediately below.

'Nancy!' A different voice shouted. She looked down to see Philip on the pavement with Hans standing beside him.

'You mad woman. What are you doing up there?'

'I'm stuck out here,' she said in a stage whisper. 'There's no door handle to get back inside.'

'Don't move,' Philip said.

'The men in my life are very good at dishing out obvious advice,' she muttered to Mimi, who was looking as bemused at her behaviour as Philip and Hans. The door opened behind Mimi, and Monsieur Martin, the cafe owner, appeared.

'What are you doing, Nancy?' he asked.

'Funnily enough, you're the third person to ask me that today.'

'Don't move. I'll get help.'

'It's ok. Philip's on his way,' she said as he went back inside with Mimi trotting after him.

Philip was taking a long time. Hans was still in the street.

'Won't be long now,' he yelled. She waved. 'I'm fine. It's quite nice up here.' Or it would be if she wasn't afraid of getting a ticking off from Madame Dubois.

The door opened behind her.

'Quick,' Philip said. 'Before her ladyship spots you.'

'I thought she was tied up with a client?' Nancy said as innocently as she could.

Philip gave her a serious look. 'We'll discuss it downstairs. Let's get you out of here.'

When they reached the kitchen, Philip stopped Nancy from walking into the shop. 'Not so fast. Why were you nosing around upstairs? That's the quickest way to get the sack around here. Why do you think there's a long list of crossed-out names?' he said, tapping the drinks list on the cupboard.

'I wasn't being nosey. I was rescuing Mimi.'

'Who prefers to relax in a specific room upstairs,' Philip said with his arms folded.

'The red one, you mean.'

'Hmm,' he said. 'I guess you understand the bespoke bindings part of the business now.'

'I guess I do. Why didn't you explain when I asked before?'

'I wasn't sure how broad-minded you were. The last shop assistant who found out walked out immediately and never came back. I didn't want you to do the same. You're not going to, are you?' He sounded worried.

'Bespoke Bindings is none of my business, is it? And I need the money.'

'Good.' He looked relieved. 'I think you owe Hans a thank you. He's in the shop.'

'I suppose so.' That was going to be awkward after she'd all but ignored him yesterday.

'I'll make some fresh tea,' Philip said.

Nancy went out onto the shopfloor, grateful to Philip for staying out of the way. Hans was half-heartedly looking at the bestsellers' table. He looked up when she walked over to him.

Just get it over and done with, Nancy! 'Thank you for fetching Philip.'

'That's ok. Were you really going to jump across to the other balcony?' he asked.

'If I'd been wearing trousers, it would have been easy.'

'It's frighting being friends with you,' he said.

'You mean "frightening". Though "scary" would be an even better word,' she said.

'Ok. It's scary being friends with you. And I'm missing our English lessons. I obviously still need them.' He smiled at her.

How she loved that smile. She was still annoyed about Wednesday's rejection, but it had been a lonely evening without their regular chat yesterday. And surely it was better to have Hans in her life as a friend than no Hans at all. 'A walk in the park would be good today with this hot weather - if you're free when I finish here, of course?' she suggested.

He looked pleased. 'I will look forward to that very much. I'll meet you in the café.'

'You're back late today,' Olivia said, looking up from her magazine as Nancy walked into the flat.

Nancy checked her watch. 'It's my usual time.'

'Only if you've been giving Hans an English lesson. I thought those were cancelled now.'

'They were, but they're back on again.'

Olivia looked surprised. 'And you tell me off for going back to Pierre.'

'That's completely different. Hans and I have never been a couple. He helped me out today, so I decided to forgive him for leading me on.'

'You did? And how did he help you exactly?'

Nancy was mentally and physically exhausted. She'd already been through the story of how and what she'd discovered today with Hans. She'd much prefer to update Olivia after having something to eat and a rest. 'It's a long story. I'll tell you tomorrow. It's Friday night. Shouldn't you be out with Pierre?'

'Pierre is visiting a restaurant this evening with his brother. They're thinking of investing in it. My opinion isn't required, apparently, so I've got all night to listen to your story.'

Nancy sighed. 'I'm really sorry.'

'About Pierre dismissing me for the evening or you not feeling up to distracting me with something interesting? If it's the latter, will a glass of wine help?' Olivia asked, getting up and heading towards the fridge.

22

Madame Dubois was working in the shop when Nancy arrived the following morning. 'Ah, the very person,' she said, looking over her specs at her. 'Can you come into the office, please? Carol can mind the shop for a few minutes.'

They both looked at Carol, who had her head in a hardback copy of *Pride & Prejudice*. 'Carol!' Madame Dubois shouted. 'Please put down Mr Darcy for a few minutes. We're leaving you in charge.'

Carol dropped the book in surprise. 'Sorry, Madame,' she said, picking it up and scuttling behind the till.

Nancy followed Madame Dubois into the back room.

'Take a seat, Nancy.'

Madame Dubois settled into her old captain's chair behind the desk while Nancy sank down into the low chair in front of it. Given how perfect the rest of Madame Dubois's furniture was, Nancy wondered if she deliberately kept this chair's upholstery saggy so she could intimidate whoever was sitting in it. It certainly felt as if Madame Dubois was towering over her.

Madame Dubois raised an eyebrow. 'About yesterday afternoon. Is there anything you want to share with me?'

How much did she know? *Keep it vague, Nancy.* 'Were you thinking of anything in particular?'

'A little bird tells me you were admiring the view across the street from the second floor?'

Had Philip grassed on her? He'd seemed keen to keep her secret. 'Really?' Nancy kept it non-committal.

'Monsieur Martin said he wanted to thank you for rescuing the lovely Mimi.'

Not Philip, then. 'Mimi decided to visit your apartment. I thought I better evict her.'

'But not before she left some cat hair in one of my rooms. My client didn't appreciate my sneezing and snotty nose.'

'Which room?' Nancy asked as innocently as she could.

'Never take up acting, Nancy. It's quite obvious you know exactly which room I'm referring to.'

'I got her out as quickly as possible,' Nancy said.

Madame Dubois leaned back in her chair. 'But she shouldn't have been there in the first place. How did she get in?'

'She opened that door herself.'

'You expect me to believe that?'

'It's true, I promise. She must have stood up on her hind legs and pulled down the handle. We used to have a cat at home that could do that. Cats can be quite clever when they want to be.'

'Are you sure you weren't being nosey?'

'Cross my heart.'

'Hmm. So what did you think?'

'Of what?'

'Of my special room.'

'Well, I've not seen anything quite like it in Ideal Home magazine.'

Madame Dubois laughed. 'No. I don't think it's a style of decor that's currently in vogue, not outside the bespoke binding community anyway.' She leaned forward in her chair.

'I'm pleased you came back today. I've lost a few assistants once they realised what was happening ustairs.'

'It's not for me to judge.'

'I appreciate you taking that understanding attitude. I have a proposition for you.'

Nancy felt nervous. What could she mean?

'My bespoke binding business keeps me very busy.' Madame Dubois raised an eyebrow. 'Too busy, but I don't like to let my clients down, so I've been searching for a suitable apprentice for a while. Would that interest you?'

Nancy hadn't anticipated that at all. 'It's not my sort of thing.'

'It doesn't have to be. In fact, it's better if it's not. You strike me as the sort of girl who doesn't take any nonsense from men. I think you'd take to it very well.'

'Well, I ….'

'It's all legal if that's what's worrying you. I don't have sex with them. I'll train you, of course. And I'll pay you handsomely.'

Nancy thought about the extra money she owed Patty. 'How handsomely?'

'Let's say 40 francs net for an hour's session.'

Nearly eight times the hourly rate for shop work! She'd only need to stick it out for ten sessions, and she'd have all the cash she needed for Patty.

But it was still a highly unusual job. And it sounded as if Madame Dubois had unsuccessfully tried to fill the position before. 'How about 50 francs an hour?' Nancy suggested.

Madame Dubois smiled. 'I like your style, Nancy. Shall we split the difference and say 45?'

So, it had been worth negotiating. 'I'm willing to settle for 45 francs with a review after ten sessions.'

Madame Dubois held out her hand to shake Nancy's. 'That's a deal. I need your absolute discretion, of course. This isn't the sort of information that you should share with anyone. No one else needs to know what goes on upstairs here.'

'No, of course not,' Nancy said, worried now about what she'd already said to Olivia and Hans.

23

'It fits perfectly,' Madame Dubois stood back, admiring Nancy's new look. 'I thought we were a similar size.'

Nancy looked at her reflection in the mirror in Madame Dubois's dungeon. No one would recognise her with the heavy make-up, the leather skirt, thigh-high patent leather boots and the tight bodice that made her look like she'd got decent-sized boobs. She hoped no one who knew her recognised her, anyway. It had seemed like a good idea when she'd accepted Madame Dubois's offer last week, but now it was becoming a reality she felt uncharacteristically nervous.

'But you do need to get the hang of walking in those heels,' Madame Dubois frowned as Nancy walked across the room for the third time. 'You're supposed to intimidate clients, not remind them of a foal trying to stand for the first time.'

'This tight skirt isn't making it easy.' Nancy said, pulling it up slightly to see if that helped. 'And I'm worried my boobs will fall out.'

'Take the outfit home tonight and practise until you look like you're on the catwalk.'

'But what about now?'

'Don't move around much. You'll be fine. Henri knows this is a practice run.'

There was a gentle tap on the door. 'Can I come in?' a man's voice called out.

'Whenever you're ready,' Nancy replied.

'No, no, no,' Madame Dubois grabbed Nancy's shoulders and looked her straight into her eye. 'Forget about being polite. In this room, you are in charge. Henri is paying to be shouted at. Try again.'

'Get in here now!' Nancy yelled aggressively.

'Much better,' Madame Dubois smiled.

Philip was reorganising the bestsellers section when Nancy walked back into the shop, dressed in her regular clothes. He raised his eyebrows when he saw her.

'What?' she asked.

'I'm not used to seeing you with heavy black eyeliner. It's very Brigitte Bardot. It suits you,' he grinned. 'How did you get on? Did Madame Dubois show you the ropes?'

'Ha ha! Very funny.'

'Sorry, I couldn't resist. Come on, dish the dirt.'

'It was surprisingly empowering. I just remembered all those arseholes who I used to work with and imagined I was dominating them.' Which had worked quite well until Henri had shouted his safe word when she'd been imagining whipping Mr Jefferson. 'Not quite so hard next time,' he had said as he'd hobbled out of the room to get dressed.

'So, will you be getting some regular customers?' Philip asked.

'I expect so. Madame Dubois says she'll take all the new ones, and once she's made sure they're not after something more, she'll book them in with me if they're happy.'

'Are you offering any particular specialities?'

'Why? Do you want to book a session?' She looked at him seductively.

'No offence, Nancy, but you know you're not my type either as you or your alter ego. This might come in useful, though,' he grinned, handing her a hardback book about the Marquis de Sade that he'd obviously deliberately tucked away under the table.

'Sod off, Mason,' she laughed, whacking him on the backside with it.

'Ow! I predict you'll get on very well in your new role.'

Nancy put her hands on her hips. 'Make the tea!' she growled.

'Yes, mistress,' Philip laughed as he headed towards the kitchen, rubbing his right buttock.

24

Nancy arrived home that evening with her new outfit wrapped in brown paper inside a bag that Madame Dubois had given her from a fancy boutique.

'Olivia!' she called out. There was no reply. She noticed a note on the dining table. 'Gone to Pierre's. Might not be back until tomorrow, Love O xx'

Perfect. She had the apartment to herself. Nancy made herself a cheese sandwich. Then proceeded to don her new outfit, leaving the boots until last.

She emerged from her bedroom and headed for the kitchen. Her right foot went over at the ankle after just two steps. Arghh! How was anyone supposed to walk in heels this high while wearing a restrictive skirt? She waggled her foot around. No damage done. She wasn't going to let it beat her though.

She carried on slowly for a few more steps. Then the same thing happened again. This time, she lost her balance and knocked over one of the dining chairs, bashing her knee against the table leg in the process. She let out a yelp of pain while the chair crashed into the sink, knocking a plate off the draining board, which then smashed on the floorboards. 'You bastard!' She shouted. *Get a grip, Nancy. It's just a question of balance. You can ride a bike, so you can master this.*

She tried again, managing to get the whole way across the room without falling over this time, albeit not very elegantly. At least she was improving. She sat down in one of the armchairs and visualised herself sashaying across the carpet.

Let's go for it. She got out of the chair and set off towards the kitchenette, swinging her hips from side to side. It wasn't so hard after all if you believed you could do it. She arrived at the sink without any more mishaps. She carefully turned to walk back to the armchair again. Much better. She continued practising, even mastering the art of turning a corner without needing to lean on anything.

She was finishing a final circuit of the room when she heard a knock on the door. Shit! There was no way she could answer it dressed like this. There was another knock. It sounded more urgent this time. Perhaps if she kept quiet, whoever it was would think she was out and go away. She stood still, listening, hoping to hear footsteps going down the stairs.

Instead, she heard a key turn in the lock. She froze. *Don't panic! It might be Olivia returning early.* But why would she knock?

Madame Morceau walked into the room, quickly followed by Hans.

The concierge looked horrified and turned away. 'Excusez moi,' she said as she disappeared back onto the landing. It was the fastest Nancy had ever seen her move.

Hans was frozen to the spot, looking at Nancy wide-eyed. Nancy didn't know what to say.

'New boots?' Hans said.

'Yes,' Nancy replied nervously. Should she explain or try to bluff it off as trying out some new fashions? *You're a lousy liar, Nancy Smith, and Hans isn't stupid. He's probably worked it out already.* 'Would you like a cup of tea?' she asked.

Nancy changed into her normal clothes in her room, while Hans boiled the kettle. By the time she walked back into the living room, he was sitting at the dining table, slowly stirring his drink.

'You'll wear the pattern off,' Nancy said as she sat down opposite him.

Hans looked puzzled. 'The pattern is on the outside of the teacup.'

'It's one of those mad English sayings. I don't really know where it comes from.'

Hans nodded and carried on stirring, focussing on the cup in front of him. Nancy didn't know where to start. 'Why did you get Madame Morceau to unlock the door?' she asked.

'I heard a crash, and then you swore loudly. I thought someone was attacking you.'

'Oh,' she said. 'I suppose I should say thank you.'

He nodded and looked up at her. 'I assume you're helping Madame Dubois with her bespoke binding business.'

'She's asked me to become her apprentice.'

He looked concerned. 'I don't want you to go to prison.'

'I won't. Provided I don't have sex with the clients, and I have no intention of doing that, it's all above board.'

'And you're quite sure about that.'

'Yes. Madame Dubois even has a policeman and several barristers on her books, apparently.'

Hans looked thoughtful.

'I sense you disapprove,' Nancy said.

'It's none of my business, but I worry about you, that's all. I don't want any harm to come to you.'

'I'm only going to do it for a few weeks until I have enough money to pay Patty. I'll have plenty of weapons at my disposal. And there's a panic button if anything goes wrong. It rings in the shop, and there's always someone in there.'

'But it would take a minute or two for Philip to run up the stairs to help. And I doubt Carol would even notice.'

'That's why we don't have special clients on Saturdays. And Philip's quite nippy when he puts his mind to it.'

'Nippy?'

'Fast. He's a quick runner.'

'Hmmm.' Hans didn't look convinced. 'What if one day he's not nippy? Have you ever studied self-defence?'

'No. I'd love to, but I haven't had the opportunity yet.'

'I think you should.' He went back to stirring his coffee.

He was right. It would be useful. 'Do you know where I can get lessons?'

'Yes. I will teach you. I learnt in the army.'

Nancy didn't know why that surprised her. A spell in the forces would explain the way Hans carried himself, his short haircut and probably that scar, too. 'You haven't mentioned that before.'

'I didn't know you were going to need it until now.'

'That's very kind. When shall we start?'

'When are you seeing your next client?'

'Tomorrow afternoon.'

'Then we better start now.'

Hans moved one of the armchairs back against the wall to give them some space.

'Let's start with someone looking like they're going to grab your arms,' he said. 'To stop them doing that, you put your hands up in front of you like this.' He held his hands up in front of his face. 'They might respond by gripping your wrists. You do that to me now.'

Nancy held Hans' wrists firmly.

'You have a strong grip,' he said.

She raised her eyebrows. 'I've been told that before.'

He avoided her gaze. 'I get out this way,' he said, lifting one arm up and one arm down, then twisting around. 'Finish with an elbow to the groin. Obviously, we won't do that today. Your turn.'

Nancy repeated the moves that Hans had demonstrated.

'Very good,' he said as she escaped from his clutches.

'That was far too easy,' she said. 'I don't think you held me very tightly. Do it again but harder this time.'

'I don't want to hurt you,' he said.

'I know, but it won't help me if you go easy on me.'

'If you're sure,' he said, grabbing her wrists again.

'Still too loose,' she said.

He tightened his grip. It hurt this time, but she wasn't going to show it. She carried out the move again. It was harder to escape, but it still worked.

'Ta da!' she said as broke free.

'You're a quick learner,' he smiled. 'Now we will look at what to do if someone grabs you from behind. For this one, you need to finish with a punch to the side of my ribs. Use the side of your fist.' He made a fist with his hand and rubbed the side nearest to his little finger to show what he meant.

'Why the side?' she asked.

'Because it's easier to get right than a proper punch.'

Nancy nodded.

'Turn around. I'll talk you through what to do.'

Nancy did as she was told. She felt Hans' arms tighten around her shoulders and upper chest, pulling her against his body. She could feel his breath on her neck. Perhaps this wasn't such a good idea because it felt good, very good. And if she wasn't very much mistaken, Hans was enjoying it too. Hans eased away slightly. She resisted the temptation to lean back into him. *Stop imagining him kissing your neck, Nancy!*

'You need to bend down a little, twist away from me, then punch. Got that?'

'Ok,' she said, bending down and twisting. They ended up face-to-face.

'I meant the other way,' he said, backing away.

'Yes, I can see that now,' she said. This was getting more awkward by the minute.

'We'll do it again.' He grabbed her around the shoulders. This time, Nancy twisted in the opposite direction and thumped him on his rib cage.

'Argghhh!' he called out. 'Perhaps not so hard when we're practising.' He rubbed his ribs. 'Are you sure you haven't done this before?'

'My big brother taught me how to box one summer.'

'That's unusual.'

'He was fed up of me annoying him. I think it was an excuse to get revenge.'

'And did he get revenge?'

'Of course not. I was far too competitive to allow him to win.'

Hans laughed. 'I can imagine that. I think that's enough for now.'

'Yes,' she agreed. 'I don't think I could cope with any more close-quarter grappling tonight.'

The following morning, Nancy put a plate of warmed croissants in front of Olivia. 'Ooh, luxury. Feeling flush?'

'I thought we deserved a treat for a change.'

'Thank you.' Olivia's smile turned into a frown. 'Why is there a bruise on your arm?'

'Where?'

'There!' Olivia pointed to the outside of Nancy's arm just above the wrist. 'It's deep purple. It looks awful.'

Nancy looked in the mirror. It did look bad. 'I bet I caught it on a bookshelf corner or something.'

'It looks more like a thumbprint to me. And there's a matching one on your other arm. Is everything ok?'

It must have happened when during Hans' self-defence lesson last night. 'Yes, everything's fine.'

'Are you sure? Philip hasn't tried anything on, has he?'

'No. Of course not. Why would you say that?'

'It looks like someone strong grabbed both your arms.'

She wasn't going to let it go. Nancy would have to be honest. 'It was Hans, actually.'

'Hans!'

'He was teaching me self-defence.'

Olivia looked sceptical.

'It's true. He thinks with Madame Dubois's interesting customers around, I ought to be able to look after myself.' Which was almost the truth.

'I thought you said they were all well-dressed gentlemen.'

'They are, but one could still turn nasty at some point.'

'So that gives Hans an excuse to hurt you? I would never have guessed he was a man like that.'

'He isn't. He didn't do it deliberately. I told him to grip me harder because it was too easy to escape when he was doing it gently.'

Nancy rubbed her arm, remembering last night's lesson.

Olivia still didn't look convinced. 'Why are you blushing? I see I'll need to keep an eye on Hans.'

25

April had turned into May, and Nancy was enjoying her new routine: her regular bespoke binding clients were not that demanding. She enjoyed working with them now. It broke up the monotony of being in the shop. Just a couple more sessions and Nancy would have more than enough money to pay Patty. And English lessons with Hans were always a pleasurable way to end the working day.

'What have you got there?' Olivia asked when Nancy walked back into their apartment carrying some envelopes.

'It's just our post. There's a lot of it today. I've got a letter with an LA postmark. I bet that's from Eddie.'

'He's made it as far as Hollywood then?'

'He must have. And you've got a letter, too.' Nancy put Olivia's envelope on the dining table.

Olivia left the cooker and glanced at the writing on the envelope. 'It's from my darling mother. I'll read that after we've eaten.'

'And we've both got one of these.' Nancy waved a small white envelope with just her name written on the front. It must have been hand-delivered. She put Olivia's matching envelope on the table next to her mother's letter.

Olivia looked up from stirring the bolognese sauce on the hob. 'Curious. Open yours then.'

'It looks fancy. I better use a paper knife.'

'We haven't got one of those. You'll have to use a normal one.' Olivia handed her a table knife from the cutlery drawer.

Nancy slit open the top of the envelope and pulled out a printed card. 'Ooh! That's a surprise.'

'What is it?'

'It's in German, but I think I understand it. It says, "Ingrid and Dieter would like to invite," and then it has my name handwritten on it. "To their Hochzeit." The card has bells embossed on it, so does that mean wedding?'

'Let's see,' Olivia took the pan off the hob, dried her hands on her apron and took the card from Nancy.

'Yes, I think you're right. Though if you turn it over, it looks like Ingrid's translated it for us.'

'Oh yes,' Nancy laughed, reading the handwritten English on the back of the card. 'Saturday 16th May 1964. That's less than two weeks away. What's the rush?'

'Perhaps there's a little Dieter on the way? She hasn't been at work for a couple of weeks.'

'Could be. Or she's still keeping him at arm's length, and he's desperate enough for sex to agree to marrying her.'

'You cynic! They could be deeply in love. Anyway, she says there's no need to bring a friend as Hans is invited too.'

Nancy rolled her eyes. 'Matchmaking again.'

'You and Hans spend a lot of time together. And I've seen the way you glance at one another when you think no one's looking.'

Did he look at her like that? After the kiss, she thought he wasn't interested. But then there had been that moment during their self-defence lesson. *Don't get your hopes up - he's been his usual self since then. It's most likely wishful thinking on Olivia's part.*

Olivia ripped open her invitation. 'Mine says Olivia plus one.'

'Good of Ingrid to leave it open. Do you think you'll still be with Pierre?'

'I might ask him,' she grinned.

Nancy looked at the date again. 'I'll have to check with Madame Dubois. I'm supposed to be working that Saturday.'

'What time is the ceremony?'

'15:30 at 18 Rue de la Republique. Where's that?'

'I don't know. Hang on.' Olivia took a small blue map book out of a kitchen drawer. She looked up the location in the index.

'There it is,' she said, pointing to a short street on the other side of the Bois de Boulogne.

Nancy took the book from her. 'It doesn't say there's anything special there. Shouldn't it be a church or something?'

'I thought it had to be a town hall to make it legal, but they might do that beforehand, and this is just the informal ceremony afterwards.'

'It will be interesting to see how a German wedding ceremony works.'

'And it's another excuse to go dress shopping!' Olivia said gleefully.

Nancy was horrified. 'I am not coming with you this time!'

26

The day of the wedding was hot and sunny. Nancy was checking her dress looked ok when there was a knock on the apartment door.

'That must be Hans,' Olivia shouted from her bedroom. 'I forgot to tell you Pierre's going to meet us there. He's been helping his brother set up his new restaurant.'

Nancy opened the door. Hans was standing on the landing, looking very suave in a new medium blue suit. It enhanced the colour of his eyes.

'At this risk of making a terrible pun, it suits you,' Nancy said.

'As the best man, I thought I should make an effort.' He smiled as he walked in. 'Dieter's gone on ahead to make sure everything is ready.'

'You're looking hot, Hans,' Olivia said as she emerged from her bedroom.

'Really? I'm feeling just right. This lightweight material is perfect for this warm spring weather.'

Nancy decided not to explain. It might make him embarrassed. But Olivia was right, he was looking hot. The better-fitting suit emphasised his broad shoulders. She remembered admiring him in his swim shorts at the toga party, and blushed at the thought.

Hans must've noticed her face going red. 'You are also looking hot, Nancy.'

'Yes, it is quite warm in here,' she said, fanning herself with the wedding invitation.

'Are you both ready?' Hans asked. 'I have a taxi waiting outside. I thought it would make for a more pleasant journey than using the Metro. My treat.'

'Hans, you're an angel. That's really considerate.' Olivia gave him a peck on each cheek.

He looked at Nancy.

'I better show my appreciation as well,' she said. She noticed him gulp as she pecked him on his left cheek. For a moment, she thought he was going to go in for a full kiss, but he changed his mind.

He coughed uncomfortably. 'Shall we go?'

'Just a minute, I almost forgot their present.' Olivia grabbed the bag containing the bottle of champagne she'd bought that morning. 'Ready now. Lead the way.'

Dieter and Pierre were already waiting outside as the taxi drew up outside the wedding venue. Pierre embraced Olivia as if they hadn't seen one another for weeks rather than a few hours.

'Nervous?' Nancy asked Dieter.

'A little,' he said. 'I will be happier when Ingrid arrives.'

No 18 was a narrow four-storey 19th-century building. 'It looks like someone's house,' Nancy said.

Dieter looked uncomfortable. 'I am a member of a small Danish Lutheran sect. We do not have a big church in Paris. We use the living room here for our ceremonies.'

'I thought you were German?'

'I am, but my mother was Danish. She wanted me to follow her religion, so she took me to her church every Sunday.'

'Will she be here today?'

'Sadly not, my family home was bombed during the war. I am an orphan.'

'Like Hans. I'm so sorry.'

'You have no need to apologise.'

Another taxi pulled up, this time carrying Ingrid and Christa.

Hans was looking uneasy now. Nancy reached out to hold his hand to help him relax, but it seemed to have the opposite effect. 'Do you wish it was you and Christa who were getting married?' she asked him.

He looked surprised. 'No, of course not.'

'If you're sure.'

'I'm very sure,' he said. 'Let go inside.'

He led her up the stairs to the front door. His hand felt hot in hers. Something was bugging him.

Nancy glanced across at him. Beads of sweat were forming on his brow. 'You don't look well. Is there anything I can do to help?'

'It's nothing, I'll be fine in a moment.' He kept holding her hand, though.

A man in a long black cassock was waiting to greet them all. He motioned toward the door into what would've been a living room overlooking the courtyard at the back of the house. Ten chairs were laid out in two rows of five, facing an altar that looked like a dining table covered in a plain green cloth.

'Is anyone else joining us?' Nancy whispered to Hans.

'No, this is everyone. Apart from the um … priest and his assistant.'

'It's very plain, isn't it?' Nancy said, looking around the room.

'I think the church is, how do you say … It does not like to show off its wealth.'

'I would say "it's not ostentatious".'

Hans didn't try to use the new word like he usually did.

'Are you feeling worse?' Nancy asked

'I am just nervous on Dieter's behalf.'

Nancy looked at Dieter, who was standing next to Ingrid in front of the priest. Dieter didn't look worried at all now Ingrid was here. In fact, he looked delighted. He couldn't keep his eyes off Ingrid, who seemed equally besotted with him.

'I don't think you need to worry about Dieter. He's doing what we should all do: taking the opportunity to be happy now without worrying too much about the future. If it doesn't work out, what has he lost? At least he'll have some good memories to look back on.'

'You're very wise.' Hans squeezed her hand.

'You're the first person to ever say that to me,' she whispered in his ear.

The ceremony started. Nancy had no idea what was happening. Everything sounded like it was in German, which was odd for a Danish religion, but as both the bride and groom were German, perhaps that was normal. She was going to ask Olivia about it, but with such a small congregation, it would be too noticeable. She'd consult her afterwards.

They moved on to a hymn, which the priest's assistant played on a small upright piano in the corner. Nancy thought she vaguely recognised the music, but either the piano was out of tune, or the church needed to invest in more piano lessons for the assistant. Olivia joined in with the singing, somehow matching the notes of the appalling piano. Nancy winced at the unholy noise. Ingrid and Dieter didn't appear to be concerned, though. Thankfully, after one verse and one chorus, the ordeal was over.

The priest moved nearer to Ingrid and Dieter, holding an open bible. Hans stood up, pulled two rings out of his jacket pocket, put them on the bible and sat down beside Nancy again.

The priest started speaking with Ingrid and Dieter taking turns repeating what he said. It was just like Church of England marriage but in German. The priest raised his hand to bless them, and they started snogging one another's faces off. The priest had to cough to grab their attention again. He indicated the book on the table.

After they'd signed the register, the priest made a short announcement.

'What did he say?' Nancy whispered to Hans.

'The ceremony is over. They are now husband and wife.'

'Doesn't someone have to witness their signatures?'

'I don't think they've thought of that,' Hans said.

Olivia, ever the organiser, had bought a bag of rice. She got up and distributed a handful each to the rest of the guests. 'We'll throw this outside,' she said. She turned to Ingrid and Dieter. 'You two stay here while we line up on the steps.' Ingrid grinned at her new husband, who seemed more than willing to comply.

'Right, everyone. Remember to throw the rice up and not at the bride and groom.' Olivia said. The newlyweds walked down the steps together through a perfect shower of rice.

Christa pulled a small camera from her handbag. 'Photo time!' she said.

Nancy noticed Hans and Dieter exchange a glance. 'That's not a problem, is it? Surely, we've got time for one photo?'

'We don't want to block the pavement,' Dieter said.

'We'll do it on the steps then.' Christa wasn't taking no for an answer.

'You need to be in it, Christa,' Ingrid said. 'Who's going to take it?'

Pierre volunteered.

'But you need to stand with Olivia. I'm sure we can find someone else. Monsieur, excusez moi,' Ingrid shouted, waving to a man who was walking by on the opposite pavement. The man crossed the road and, after a brief conversation with Christa, took the camera.

'It's all automatic,' Christa said. 'Just look through the viewfinder and press this button here.'

He nodded. She ran back up the steps to take her place.

The passerby took two shots in quick succession and handed the camera back to Christa.

'I wish you a long and happy life together,' he said to Ingrid and Dieter as he walked off.

'Shall we go now, darling?' Dieter said to Ingrid in German. At least, that's what it sounded like to Nancy.

'Thank you all for coming,' Ingrid said before Dieter led her away.

'No wedding reception?' Nancy asked Hans.

'Dieter's booked a fancy hotel room for the two of them tonight. I expect they want to make the most of it.'

Christa said she'd got some shopping to do. 'I'm going to decorate our flat ready for when the lovebirds come home tomorrow. And buy some earplugs. Something tells me I'm not going to get much peace for a few weeks with those two in the bedroom next door,' she laughed.

'We have to go, too,' Pierre said, putting his arm around Olivia. 'It's opening night at my brother's new restaurant.'

'Enjoy!' Nancy said. She turned back to Hans.

'Just you and me then.'

He looked concerned. 'Is that a problem?'

'No. But I was hoping they'd have a party so I'd finally get a chance to find out how good a dancer you are.'

'We can go dancing if you want. I know an exclusive venue where they play the music you like.'

'I like the sound of that. Is it far?'

'Not far at all.'

'Good.' She smiled. 'Let's go.'

He waved down the next taxi that drove past. 'Rue de la Dordogne please.'

Nancy looked surprised. 'I didn't know there were any clubs in our street.'

'I said it was exclusive.' He held the taxi door open for her.

'I'm not sure I've got the right shoes on for dancing. Can I pop home and change them?' she asked.

'You can dance in your bare feet if you want.'

'It sounds very laid back, this venue.'

'It is. I hope you'll love it.'

The taxi set off. Nancy looked out of the window, trying to work out how there could be a club on their street without any evidence of music or people visiting it.

'Are you ok?' Hans asked.

'I'm just confused by this mysterious club. Is it like Brigadoon?'

It was Hans' turn to look puzzled now. 'What is Brigadoon?'

'It's a mythical Scottish village that only appears for one day every hundred years.'

He grinned back at her. 'I'm hoping it will be around more often than that.'

Nancy looked at Hans smiling next to her. 'You seem very relaxed. In fact, you're the most relaxed I've ever seen you.'

'I thought about what you said earlier, about taking a chance to be happy without worrying about the future. I need to be brave enough to do the same.'

'That sounds promising.'

He reached out and held her hand. The taxi turned the corner into their street. 'Pull up outside number 27, please,' Hans said to the driver.

'So we are going home first?'

'You'll see.' He got out of the taxi, paid the fare, then opened the main door to their apartment block and headed for the door to their stairwell. They climbed the stairs together until they reached the third floor.

'Here we are,' Hans said.

Nancy was confused. 'But this is your flat.'

'It is. And I'll be here alone now that Dieter is moving in with Ingrid.'

'I thought you said we were going dancing.'

'We are. I have a record player and records you love so we can dance with no one else to bother us. What do you think? You're not disappointed, are you?'

The idea of having Hans all to herself wasn't a disappointment. Far from it. 'It's a lovely idea.'

'There's even wine if you want it.'

'Last time we drank wine together, I scared you off.'

'That's not going to happen this evening.'

Nancy liked the way this was going. She heard the downstairs door open. It was Madame Morceau doing her daily inspection of the stairwell.

'Shall we go inside?' Hans whispered in her ear.

'Do you think the doorman will let us in?' Nancy smiled at him.

'I think he might.'

27

A while later, Nancy lay in Hans' arms, their bodies entwined in a mess of sheets on his bed.

'Who taught you how to do all that?' she asked.

'If I told you, you wouldn't believe me,' he said. 'I don't want to know who taught you either.'

'That sounds fair.'

'Ich liebe dich, Nancy,' Hans murmured in her ear as he ran his fingers through her hair.

'Ich liebe dich auch, Hans,' she replied.

She felt his body tense. Why would he object to her saying she loved him when he'd said the same to her?

'Did I pronounce that incorrectly?' Nancy asked, pulling away from him so she could see his face properly.

'No, you said it perfectly. It's just that …' He hesitated. 'It's nothing. Forget I said anything.' He stroked her face, looking intently into her eyes. 'I truly love you, Nancy. Always remember that.'

'I'm glad you changed your mind about us,' she said.

'So am I. It doesn't matter what happens next. We'll always have Paris.'

It was Nancy's turn to flinch. 'Don't say that.'

'Why not?'

'It's a famous line from *Casablanca*. Humphrey Bogart says it to Ingrid Bergman when they say goodbye forever.'

'It might have meant that in their story but not in ours.'

'I hope you're right.'

'I'm sure I am.' He kissed her gently on the neck and began working his way down her body.

'I think I can work out where you've been all night,' Olivia said as Nancy walked into their flat the following morning.

'I just came up to get a change of clothes. Hans and I are going out for breakfast.'

Olivia put down her cup of coffee. 'And what are you and the lovely Hans planning to do after that?'

Nancy raised her eyebrows.

Olivia looked bemused. 'I thought you said you weren't going to get involved with him. "No point when I'm sailing away in a few weeks", I seem to recall you saying?'

'I know, but it all got a bit intense yesterday.'

Olivia went back to her breakfast. 'It did sound that way.'

'How do you know that? I thought you were stopping at Pierre's?'

'We had an argument. I came back early.'

'How early?'

'About ten o'clock.'

'Oh.' Nancy blushed. 'I'd have been quieter if I'd known.'

'The noise you were making downstairs, I could probably have heard you from Pierre's.'

'We got carried away.' Nancy sat down at the table opposite her. 'He told me he loved me.'

Olivia stopped buttering her croissant. 'And that was enough to convince you to part with your knickers?'

Nancy grinned. 'I'd already abandoned them at that point.'

'It sounded like it was worth abandoning them. He knows what he's doing then.'

'Definitely. Better even than Billy. And he can dance.'

'Lucky you.' Olivia sucked the butter off her fingers.

'You're not going back to Pierre again, are you? I don't understand why you put up with him. What if he gets you pregnant, and you're stuck with him?'

'But he's got that rugged look that I can't resist, and he makes me laugh. He gets so downcast when I dump him, I feel guilty if I don't take him back.'

'You can't keep a man because he will look fantastic in the wedding photos, and he'll inherit a chateau when you're 50.'

'And a vineyard. Don't forget the vineyard.'

Nancy rolled her eyes. 'I'm sure there are plenty of eligible men in France who already have their own vineyard. Why settle for one who's waiting for Daddy to pop his clogs before you can get your hands on the vintage Chardonnay.'

'You don't get Chardonnay in the Loire Valley.'

'I apologise for my ignorance of viticulture, but you know exactly what I mean.'

'We're supposed to be discussing you and Hans. I presume now he's declared his undying love for you, you're officially a couple now?'

'I think we might be,' Nancy smiled.

28

Nancy relaxed in a chair in the café in the Bois de Boulogne. She'd positioned herself so the sun was shining on her face. A little vitamin D wouldn't go amiss - she was looking paler than she usually did in July, probably because she wasn't spending as much time outdoors now she and Hans were officially together. Not that she was complaining about that. The last six weeks had been bliss. With Dieter living with Ingrid now, Nancy had as good as moved in with Hans, though he hadn't given her any keys yet.

She looked at her watch. Hans was usually here by now. Something must have come up at work.

The waiter approached her table. 'Another coffee?'

'Yes, please,' she replied in French. 'Actually, make that two. I'm sure my friend will be here any minute now.'

'Certainly, Madame.'

She smiled to herself. She wouldn't have been able to hold that conversation in French when she'd first arrived in Paris. What a difference four months had made. Leaving Coventry had been an excellent decision.

She wasn't so sure about her next major move, though. She'd received a letter from Patty yesterday containing details of what to bring with her to Portsmouth in two months' time. It made the whole round-the-world trip seem real, along with the less appealing prospect of leaving Hans for six months. Olivia reckoned the odds of their relationship surviving being apart for that long were pretty slim.

Nancy was hoping to talk to Hans today about how they might make it work. She'd proved popular with Madame Dubois's bespoke bindings clientele which meant she'd managed to save up enough money to pay for him to fly out to meet her when they docked in Cape Town, assuming his employer would give him some time off. But, he had kept changing the subject whenever she'd tried to float the idea this week.

The waiter returned with their coffees. Where was Hans?

Nancy ended up drinking both cups of coffee while she waited for Hans to show up.

She must've misunderstood their arrangement to meet, but it was their usual routine, so that didn't make sense. She would've remembered if they'd agreed to do something different. She walked back to their apartment building and knocked on the door of his flat, but there was no answer. She put her ear to the door and listened. She couldn't hear anything inside.

'Hans!' She called and banged on the door again. Still no reply.

There is bound to be a perfectly simple explanation. She ran up the final flight of stairs and let herself into her flat.

Olivia was there cooking dinner with Pierre. 'Are you ok?' Olivia asked.

'Has Hans been in touch?'

Olivia shook her head. 'No, should he have been?'

'He didn't turn up at the cafe today. We were planning to go for our usual walk after work.'

'Have you checked if he's left a note in the postbox?' Pierre suggested.

'No. He usually puts a note under our door if he wants to tell me anything.'

'Definitely no note here.' Olivia said.

'I'll check downstairs, just in case.' Nancy ran back down the stairs and across the courtyard to the postboxes. There was nothing in there either.

What next? Dieter might know.

She headed over the road to Christa, Ingrid and Dieter's.

Christa buzzed her up.

'We don't know where Dieter is either,' she said as Nancy exited the lift on the second floor. 'Come in.'

Ingrid was sitting on the sofa, her head in her hands. She looked up at Nancy, her eyes all red and puffy. 'I know something is wrong. I feel it inside. Dieter was meant to meet me for lunch today, but he didn't show up. And now he's not come home this evening either. It's so unlike him.'

'Could he be busy at the laboratory?'

'I've tried calling there several times this afternoon, but it only gives the 'number unobtainable' dial tone. It always used to work. I can't understand it.'

'I guess the fact that they've both disappeared at the same time means it's more likely they're doing something together,' Nancy said, trying to see the positive side of the situation.

'I suppose so, but what are they doing that's so important or urgent that they can't contact us to say where they are? And why are they doing something together on a day when they should both be at their respective jobs?' Ingrid said.

Nancy had no suggestions.

29

Nancy hung around at Christa and Ingrid's until 11 pm, thinking that if there was any news, Ingrid was more likely to be informed first as she was Dieter's wife.

Olivia and Pierre had already gone to bed when Nancy got home.

She gulped down a large glass of Olivia's wine in a bid to make herself tired. But it didn't work. After a restless night, she finally gave up trying to sleep at 7 am and got dressed.

She headed down the stairs to Hans' flat in case he'd returned overnight. She knocked several times on the door. There was still no reply.

She was just about to head back upstairs when she heard footsteps below. *Don't get too excited - they sound like a woman's.* Ingrid appeared on the landing. Judging by the dark circles under her eyes, she hadn't slept either. 'Any news?' Nancy asked.

'No, I was hoping you would have heard something.'

'Nothing at all.'

'I'm going to call in sick,' Ingrid said. 'I haven't slept, so it's not an untruth. I'll phone around the hospitals later.'

'Let me know if you hear anything,' Nancy said, giving her a hug.

Olivia was making coffee when Nancy walked back into the flat. 'Still no Hans?'

'No. And Ingrid hasn't heard from Dieter either. Do you think we should report them missing?'

'I doubt the police will do anything until they've been gone for more than 24 hours.'

'Which will be lunchtime for Dieter,' Nancy said.

'Are you going to work?'

'I may as well. Hans will come looking for me there if he wants to find me.'

Later that morning, Madame Dubois cornered Nancy in the back room of the shop. 'Will you be alright with Monsieur Laurent this afternoon? You've been drifting around the shop like a wet weekend all morning.'

'I'm sorry I've been distracted. Hans has gone missing.'

'Have you fallen out with him?'

'No. We've been getting on really well. His friend Dieter has gone AWOL too.'

Madame Dubois looked concerned. 'Have you checked the hospitals in case they've been injured? The way everyone drives round here, I'm amazed more people don't get run over. '

'Dieter's wife has already phoned around. She popped in just now to tell me. There's no sign of either of them.'

'It must be worrying, but I'm sure there will be a simple explanation. What about his employer - have they heard anything from him?'

'I don't actually know who his employer is.' Which sounded ridiculous given how close they'd become. Hans still avoided talking about his work.

'You could report him missing?'

'Olivia thought it was too soon.'

'Possibly. If you want to take this afternoon off I can always phone Monsieur Laurent to ask him to rebook?'

'That's very kind of you but I'll be fine. It will take my mind off it.'

After she left the bookshop at the end of the day, Nancy looked into the café opposite, hoping that Hans might be sitting there ready to surprise her. But there was no sign of him.

He might have gone directly to the Bois de Boulogne? Her inner voice was more optimistic than she was today. She headed to the park, but he wasn't at their usual cafe either. One of the waiters came over to her.

'Have you seen Hans?' she asked.

He shook his head. 'Not since you were here two days ago. Your usual?'

'No thanks. I better not stay.'

He looked at her sympathetically. He was probably thinking they'd had some sort of argument.

'Hopefully, we'll see you both tomorrow,' he said kindly.

'Hopefully.'

Nancy hurried back to her apartment building. She checked the postbox - it was empty. She ran up the stairs to Hans' flat and banged on the door. Still no reply. 'Where the bloody hell are you?' She shouted in frustration, leaning her head against the door.

She heard Olivia's voice call out to her over the bannister. 'Ingrid and Christa are here.'

'There's no news, though,' Olivia added when Nancy looked up expectantly.

'What do we do now?' Nancy asked as she walked into the living room.

'I went to the police station this afternoon and reported them missing,' Ingrid said.

'What did they say?'

'They took all the details and said they'd be in touch if they heard anything. So I guess we just have to wait.'

'I'm not very good at waiting,' Nancy said as she took the cup of tea Olivia offered her. 'I wonder if Madame Morceau would let us into Hans' flat? There might be a clue there.'

Or Hans lying there unconscious or worse. *Why didn't you think of that yesterday?*

'You could ask. She can only say no.' Olivia said.

'I'll come with you,' Ingrid offered.

She followed Nancy downstairs and across the courtyard to the concierge's tiny lodge.

Madame Morceau was sitting by her window. She opened her door. 'Oui?'

Nancy explained the situation. 'Please could you let us into his flat so we can check if Hans is there?'

'He's not there,' she said.

'But you don't know that for sure.'

'I do. The flat is empty apart from the basic furniture that belongs there. A woman came to take away his things this morning.'

'What woman?'

Madame Morceau shrugged. 'I didn't ask her name. She had the necessary paperwork. She was from the company that rented the apartment. They wanted to terminate the rental agreement early. She paid the remaining rent, so I let her in. She left with a suitcase half an hour later. I checked everything was ok in there and locked up.'

'Did she say why he'd left?'

'No, and I didn't ask either. It's best not to ask too many questions in this job.'

'What did she look like?'

'Thirty-ish. Short dark hair, apart from a streak of white at the front. Smartly dressed.' She sounded exactly like the woman Nancy had seen with Hans in the Louvre all those weeks ago.

'What's the name of the company?' Ingrid asked.

Madame Morceau reached inside her lodge and produced a letter typed on headed paper. Nancy quickly read it. The letter requested that the rental agreement be terminated exactly as Madame Morceau had said. The company name was Fischer Exportations. She'd never heard of them, but their address was near the bookshop.

She showed the letter to Ingrid. 'It's too late to go there now. No one will be there at this time,' Ingrid said.

'We'll go first thing tomorrow.'

30

Nancy had slept deeply for the first time since Hans had gone missing. Madame Morceau's revelation yesterday had been shocking, and it hadn't stopped her worrying about where Hans was, but at least it was less likely that he was lying dead in an alley somewhere.

She got out of bed and almost fell over as she walked into the lounge.

Olivia rushed over to grab her. 'What's wrong with you?'

'I came over all faint.'

'That's not surprising, considering you haven't eaten properly for two days. I'll cook you some scrambled eggs.'

'Oh god, no. I can't face that. Tea will do.'

'Are you sure?'

'Yes, honestly.' She headed for the dining table and dropped into one of the chairs. *Deep breaths, Nancy. You'll be fine.*

'What's the plan then?' Olivia asked while she filled the kettle.

'I'm going to go to Fischer Exportations before I go to work. Ingrid's coming with me, in case I need her German skills. We're going to demand to know what's going on.'

Olivia put the tea in front of Nancy and sat opposite her, nursing a cup of coffee. 'Is that wise?' she asked.

'I don't think it's unreasonable to want to know why they've sent my boyfriend away without giving him enough time to leave me a note.'

'He might be planning to write to you from Berlin or wherever he's gone?'

'If you suddenly had to drop everything and go home, wouldn't you get a message to Pierre somehow? Not leave him wondering whether you were alive or dead?'

'It is odd. But that's not the only odd thing.'

'What do you mean?'

'I probably should've said this before, but you don't think Hans is a spy, do you?'

Olivia had outrageous ideas sometimes, but this one was at a whole new level of ridiculousness.

'What on earth makes you say that?'

'It's just I have a feeling his friend Dieter is.'

'What? Cute little Dieter?'

'Cute little Dieter has Ingrid eating out of his hand. She's even more besotted with him now they're married. I'm surprised she makes it to work some mornings after her accounts of what they get up to every night. I think she's been smuggling out papers for him.'

'How do you know that?'

'She accidentally dropped some on the pavement when we were walking back from work together last week. I helped her pick them up before the wind blew them away. It looked like she'd folded them up and tucked them in her bra.'

'What makes you think they were for Dieter?'

'We aren't supposed to bring work home. Any work you haven't finished by the end of the day is supposed to be locked away in your drawer until the following morning.'

'Not tucked down your cleavage?' Nancy said.

'Exactly.'

'Did you ask her why?'

'She said she was behind with her translation work, and she needed to do some at home to catch up.'

'Ingrid always complains that her boss is a slave driver. I can imagine she might have to sneak work home with her to make sure she doesn't fall behind. What's that principle - Occam's Razor? The simplest explanation is usually the best one. And Dieter's a biologist. Why would a biologist want papers about missiles or whatever it is you're working on there?'

'He wouldn't. Unless he's not really a biologist.'

'It all sounds far-fetched to me.' Nancy tried to process it all. Could it be true? 'Let's just say your theory is correct, and Dieter is a spy. Who's he spying for? The Russians?'

'Christa says he has a Berlin accent. What if he's from East Berlin?'

Nancy's mind started racing. Dieter couldn't be East German. He'd known Hans since they were children. Whenever they were together, they exchanged those sorts of knowing looks that you only shared if you'd been friends for years. Surely they couldn't be faking that? Though they could have lived on what were now different sides of the wall. 'Even if Dieter is a spy, it doesn't mean Hans is as well. Let's face it. He's not getting any useful information from me. I haven't got access to NATO secrets. Why didn't he make a play for you if that's what he and Dieter are after?'

'I don't fancy him. And I've always been in a relationship with Pierre since Hans gave up pursuing Christa's affections. You might not have access to military secrets, but you're very good at describing the men who frequent Madame Dubois's private apartments.'

'Why would Madame Dubois's kinky clientele be of any use to the East Germans?'

'We know at least one of them is a government minister. I can imagine the threat of exposing someone's taste for being tied up and whipped could make them give up some very useful secrets.'

Nancy was stunned. Hans always liked hearing about the men who visited the bookshop. He made a point of asking her most days what had happened and who had visited. Was that why he'd come into the bookshop the day she first met him? All these weeks, she'd been falling in love with him, and she thought he'd been falling for her too when really he was just pumping her for information. 'So you think Hans is blackmailing them?'

'Not necessarily Hans. In fact, it's very unlikely to be Hans. I guess he feeds the information back to his East German handlers, and they do the rest.'

An image of the woman with the white streak in her hair floated into Nancy's mind. Could she be his handler? 'No! I refuse to believe it. You've read too many thrillers.'

'You're the one who reads spy stories. I prefer a good old-fashioned bodice ripper myself.'

As outlandish as Olivia's idea was, it did make sense of a lot of things. Had Hans been using her? He was a bastard if he was.

'Are you still going to his offices?' Olivia asked.

'Absolutely. I need to know what's going on.'

Nancy and Ingrid had no trouble finding Fischer Exportations' address. It was a single tatty black door next to a barber's.

'I can't see a name plaque,' Ingrid said.

'No, it's very nondescript,' Nancy said. *Just the sort of door a spy agency might hide behind.* For god's sake, even her inner voice had signed up to Olivia's theory now. 'Their offices must be upstairs. Let's see, shall we.' Nancy went up to the door and pressed the bell next to it. They waited for a minute, but no one answered.

'Wouldn't you have a warehouse if you were an exporter?' Ingrid asked.

'They might have one of those as well.' Nancy pressed the bell again, holding it down this time.

'I'm coming, I'm coming,' a frustrated voice yelled in French. 'Does nobody have any patience any more?' A man holding a broom opened the door. Nancy released the bell push. 'We're looking for Fischer Exportations.'

The man shrugged. 'They're not here any more. They moved out yesterday, and I'm having to clear up the mess. Bits of shredded paper everywhere.' He went to shut the door, but Nancy was too quick for him. She put her hand out and held the door open.

'Do you know a Hans Schmidt?'

'No.' He looked fed up.

'Or a Dieter Lehrmann?' Ingrid asked.

'No.'

'Did they leave a forwarding address?'

'Unfortunately not. Now, if you don't mind, I have work to do.' He slammed the door in Nancy's face.

'What next?' Ingrid asked.

'I have absolutely no idea.'

Part Three

February 2020

31

Mary finished pouring a mug of coffee in her tiny cafe on the Dashford seafront. Even though it was only just gone noon, it would have to be the last one of the day. After the severe weather warning on the radio this morning, she planned to close early before the sea turned wild.

She headed outside to where Nancy was sitting at a table, wrapped up in a thick padded coat. She seemed to be mesmerised by the large waves breaking on the beach.

'We're expecting a storm,' Mary said as she put Nancy's second mug of black coffee down on the table in front of her.

'Aren't we all,' Nancy replied, sighing.

What an odd thing to say. But then everything about Nancy's presence here was odd. It was the first time she'd visited in fifteen years at least. Mary shuddered at the memory of Nancy's dog, Basil, whimpering over his broken leg. Stupid animal, running out behind Mary's car like that. At least he'd survived. Why had Nancy suddenly decided to forgive and forget, particularly today when it was hardly ideal weather for sitting outside? And why was she drinking coffee? In all the years Mary had known Nancy, she had never seen so much as a drop of coffee pass Nancy's lips.

'I'm going to bring the tables and chairs in,' Mary announced.

Nancy looked at her. 'I want to sit here for a while longer.'

'I'll be locking up in ten minutes. You're alright until then. Is that coffee ok? You're not normally a coffee drinker.'

'It seemed appropriate today,' Nancy said, slowly turning the mug around

What did she mean by that? 'Is there anything you want to talk about?'

Nancy shook her head and looked away.

Fine. If that's how it was going to be, she could suit herself. Mary busied herself collecting the tables and chairs and putting them in the storage area behind the cafe. She carried on until they were all packed away, apart from the table and chair Nancy was using.

Mary looked across at Nancy again. She was ignoring her coffee now. She looked freezing cold. Surely, a woman in her mid-70s shouldn't be sitting outside in a high wind on a cold winter's day. Mary tried again. 'Can I get you anything else?'

'I'm sorry?'

Mary repeated her question slowly and more loudly.

Nancy huffed. 'No, thank you. And there's no need to talk to me as if I'm senile. I'd appreciate it if you left me alone.'

The wind wasn't the only thing that was sharp today. Mary retreated to the safety of the café. Perhaps she should phone Em. She took her phone out of her apron pocket.

Em answered immediately.

'It's Mary. Is Nancy ok?'

'I think so. Why do you ask?'

'She's sitting outside my café nursing a mug of coffee and staring out to sea.'

'In this weather?' Em obviously thought it was odd, too.

'Exactly.'

'Did she drive down? I don't remember hearing her go out.'

Mary looked around the corner of the cafe at the car park. 'I can't see her car.'

'I'll come and fetch her.'

Em got out of the car and headed towards Mary's cafe. Nancy stood up as she approached.

'If you're after a sludgy coffee or you want to be interrogated about your personal life, you'll have to go to Fisherman's Arms. Mary's just shutting up shop.' Nancy told Em, a hint of disapproval in her voice. 'Though they're not quite as nosy in the Fisherman's Arms.'

Mary scowled at her. 'The last big storm we had, waves were crashing right where you were sitting. You'd have been washed out to sea. I don't want your sons or anyone else, for that matter, suing me for negligence,' she said as she picked up the small table that Nancy had been sitting at. 'And my coffee is not sludgy. People come from miles around to drink it. You should have stuck to tea.'

There was obviously still no love lost between the two women, which made it all the more odd that Nancy was here.

The wind was seriously picking up now. Mary struggled to hold the table as a gust caught it like a sail. Em dashed over to help her.

'No, no, no,' Mary said. 'I'll manage. I don't want you to get injured in your condition. Congratulations, by the way.' Another gust helpfully blew her into the storage area.

Someone else who already knew Em's news then. 'Did Nancy tell you?'

'No, I did not.' Nancy looked quite affronted by the suggestion.

Em picked up the remaining chair and handed it to Mary.

'Paul at the Gallery whispered it to me a couple of weeks ago.' Mary said as she put it away and locked up. 'Is it common knowledge now?'

'I guess so.' Em was getting used to her pregnancy being an open secret. How on earth did Paul know? Had Jack let slip something to him as well? But she'd have to follow that up with Jack later. Right now, she needed to persuade Nancy to go home.

'Why are you here?' Nancy asked Em. 'You said you were going straight home after you'd finished the admin?'

'I thought you could do with a lift home before the rain set in. Mary was concerned about you.'

'I'm not that fragile. I'm perfectly capable of walking back up to the Grange. I've done it in all weathers for the last 70 years. You're not turning into Nigel, are you? That boy is still desperate to lock me away in an old people's home.'

Nancy's eldest son, Nigel, always underestimated his mother's capabilities from the safety of his home 3,000 miles away in New York. Em, however, didn't. She was taken aback. She didn't normally get the rough side of Nancy's tongue. She was tempted to let her get on with it, but something must be seriously wrong to put her in this mood.

'It's nothing to do with age,' Em said. 'We'd all struggle to walk back up the hill in this weather. And several trees on the wooded part of the route don't look stable. Two of them came down last time we had a high wind. I'd never forgive myself if you got struck down by one of them.'

Nancy grudgingly seemed to see the sense in what Em was suggesting. 'Ok then. Thank you.'

'The car's over there by the ticket machine.' Em said, handing Nancy the keys. 'I just need to ask Mary something.'

When Nancy was out of earshot, Em turned to Mary. 'Has she said what's bothering her?'

'She wouldn't tell me anything. But she was reading a letter a few minutes ago.'

'Was it from Germany?'

Mary shrugged. 'I've no idea, but I did notice it started "My darling Nancy".'

'Is everything ok?' Em asked Nancy as they drove up the hill back to Dashford Grange.

Nancy debated whether to share any of the many thoughts racing around her head. She didn't want to be quizzed until she got things straight in her own mind. If there was anyone she was going to share the news with first, it should be Olivia. She would be more helpful in this situation.

'I'm fine, thank you.'

'If you're sure. You don't seem your usual self to me.'

'Perhaps it's the threat of the incoming storm making me feel out of sorts.' Nancy sensed Em didn't believe that. She deliberately looked out of the passenger window so Em couldn't catch her eye.

They continued in silence until Em turned the car into the drive leading up to the Grange.

'Do you want me to stay with you this afternoon?' Em offered. 'I've still got plenty of admin work to do.'

That was the last thing Nancy wanted. She'd planned her next step, and it required being left alone to use the laptop in peace.

'I'll be fine. You go home and put your feet up. You need to take it much easier now,' she said, attempting to be her usual cheery self.

Nancy got out of the car and let herself into the house, aware that Em was watching her. She stood on the doorstep and turned back, smiling and waving. Em took the hint and drove away.

Time to spring into action. Nancy collected the laptop from the desk in the kitchen and took it into her study just in case Em found an excuse to come back.

She took the letter out of her pocket again. It must be genuine. Why would anyone take the trouble to fake someone's handwriting when they could easily type it on a computer and just copy the signature instead? And there was something about how the writer used words and phrases that was instantly familiar, even after 56 years apart.

But if Hans wanted to get in touch again, she needed to make sure it genuinely was him and find out what he'd been up to since she last saw him. For all her love of adventure, she didn't like surprises.

He hadn't given his address, just a phone number. She started by searching for that to see if it was his.

Nothing came up. He must be ex-directory, but most people were these days, so that didn't prove a thing.

She searched for his name. 54 million results. Hardly surprising. Why couldn't she have fallen for someone with a less common name?

She tried "Hans Schmidt Berlin" instead.

That narrowed it down to a mere 15 million results. It was like looking for a needle in a haystack. She clicked on the images option in case there was a photo of him. There were many men of all ages, but none looked familiar. Though he would be 80 now. Would she recognise him from a recent photo?

And what if he wasn't in Berlin? She looked more closely at the postmark. It was illegible, so there was no help there. But the postage stamp was German. That narrowed it down, but Germany was a big country.

She was just about to try searching for "Hans Schmidt importer" when Olivia phoned. 'What's wrong?' she asked as soon as Nancy answered.

'Who says anything is wrong?'

'I've had reports you were behaving strangely this morning. Jack texted me.'

'If you call wanting to be on my own, behaving strangely, then yes, I suppose I have.'

'Has someone upset you? You're not normally one for seeking solitude.'

'No, I had a letter out of the blue.'

'Ooh. Not bad news, I hope.'

'No, it surprised me, that's all.'

'How intriguing. Are you going to tell me who it's from?'

Nancy laughed. There was no way Olivia would let the topic go until she got every piece of information out of her, which, in this instance, would be helpful. 'Hans.'

'Hans?' Oliva sounded shocked. 'The amazing vanishing Hans?'

'Yes. How many other people named Hans do you know?'

'Good god, after all this time. What did he say?'

'That he misses me. He always has.'

'He should have thought of that before he did a moonlight flit.' Olivia hadn't had a good word to say about Hans since his disappearance, not that they'd discussed him in many years. Nancy had tried to forget about him completely, but there was always a nagging doubt in the back of her mind that something bad had happened to him, and they should've done more to find him. Olivia didn't buy that at all. She just thought he was, at best, an idiot and, at worst, a lying bastard.

'Apparently, there's an explanation for that. He wants to meet me to tell me what happened. He suggested I phone him so we could make arrangements.'

Olivia sighed. 'And why couldn't he tell you in his letter? Or over the phone? Are you sure it's not some sort of scam?'

'No, I'm not sure. His letter contains lots of detail about what we did in Paris, but that might be a deliberate attempt to make me think it's genuine. If he kept a diary, someone could have found it and used the information to fool me. That's why I want to find out what he's been up to since 1964. The letter says he waited until his wife died before he contacted me. Other than that, he doesn't say how he's spent the last 50-odd years. You've not kept in touch with Christa or Ingrid, have you?'

'No. I exchanged Christmas cards with Christa for a few years, but they stopped when the children were young. Have you tried looking on Facebook?'

'Not yet. But I guess it will be a similar story there. There are so many Hans Schmidts in the world.'

'What you need is a professional. The private detective I used to spy on Isabella might be able to help. '

Nancy remembered him doing an excellent job on Jack's ex-wife. 'Does he cover Germany?'

'I've no idea, but I assume he's got contacts who can help if he doesn't. I'll find his details and text you.'

Later that afternoon, Nancy walked up the old, narrow servants' stairs into the attic rooms at the top of the house.

There were full with piles of boxes of old papers and discarded furniture from decades ago. She ought to sort through it all. There might be some hidden gems she could reinstate downstairs or sell. But she'd been saying that ever since she inherited the house in the 1970s. It wasn't fair to leave all this for Mark and Nigel to sort through when she eventually shuffled off this mortal coil. However, that wasn't why she was up here today.

Olivia's private detective had got straight back to Nancy after she'd texted him. He couldn't help, he said, but he recommended a company in Berlin and gave her their email address. After exchanging a few messages, they'd agreed on a price. She'd given them all the information she had on Hans, including a photo of the envelope the letter had arrived in, in case they could decipher the postmark. But they'd also asked if she had a photo of him, and she'd only ever had one of those.

She moved a few boxes out of the way, coughing at the clouds of dust she was stirring up. A cardboard filing box labelled "Nancy 1972" caught her eye. She knocked the thick layer of dust off the top so it wouldn't fall on the contents, then carefully lifted the lid. Some old children's books and a photo album lay on top. But underneath, she found what she was looking for: a sheaf of letters tied up with a red ribbon. The envelope on top had "Nancy" written on it in Hans' writing. She stifled a sniffle.

You ridiculous woman, she said to herself as she undid the ribbon. The bundle contained every letter and card she'd received in Paris, including the note Hans had pushed under her door to schedule his first English lesson. She flicked through the papers until she found the envelope she was looking for.

It was a card from Ingrid and Dieter to say thank you for their wedding present. Inside the card, Ingrid had included a copy of the photo of the wedding party the passerby had taken with Christa's little camera. There they all stood, the newlyweds in the centre with Christa, Olivia and Pierre on Ingrid's side and Nancy and Hans next to Dieter.

Darling Hans. Seeing his slightly crooked smile made her heartbeat speed up. *Or you forgot to take your tablets this morning.*

He looked so young. They all did. The picture was too small to show his long blond eyelashes, but she could see them clearly in her mind's eye as she remembered the feel of his lips on hers the first time he'd kissed her by the restaurant. *Get a grip, woman. All this talk of babies must be making you sentimental in your old age.*

32

The following week, Nancy received an email from the detective agency.

Dear Mrs Farnham.

We are sorry to tell you we have been unable to find Herr Schmidt. The only Hans Schmidt with the birthdate you gave us sadly passed away at the age of 2 in 1941. We have looked for men called Hans Schmidt who are of a similar age, including those for whom Hans is a middle name, but none of them are or were importers or exporters or could have been in Paris in 1964. The telephone number you gave us for him is not publicly listed, so we have been unable to confirm to whom it belongs.

It is very unusual for us to fail to find an individual. Is there any further information you could give us?

We have attached our invoice for the work we have carried out so far. We would appreciate payment within ten working days.

Nancy reread the email. How could they have completely failed to find Hans? Their website contained lots of positive reviews and certifications, and Olivia's private detective had said he'd used them several times and always found them highly efficient. She had to assume they were correct - there was no information out there, which meant the letter was a scam after all, but her instincts told her it was genuine.

What should she do? The sensible thing would be to ignore it. *Since when have you ever done the sensible thing, Nancy Smith?* Sod it. She needed to know what was going on. It would be lunchtime in Germany now. She tapped the number he'd given into her phone and pressed the Green dial button.

She didn't have to wait long for an answer.

'Hallo.' Was it Hans? The voice didn't sound familiar. Nancy realised that she'd never spoken to Hans on the phone before, and, in any case, his voice was bound to have changed after all these years.

'Guten Tag,' she said in her best German. 'Am I speaking to Hans Schmidt?'

She heard him take a sharp intake of breath. 'Hello, Nancy,' he replied.

'How did you know it was me?'

He chuckled. That sound was familiar - wonderfully familiar. Nancy allowed herself a sigh of relief. Not a scam then - or if it was, it was Hans who was scamming her.

'I was hoping you would call,' he said. 'I was only thinking about you this morning but then I think about you often.'

'You do?'

'Yes. We had happy times together. Yes?'

'Yes, we did.'

'I often wondered how you were and what you were doing.'

Nancy opened her mouth but no sound would come out.

'Nancy?' He sounded concerned.

Pull yourself together, woman. Say something, or he'll hang up.

'Sorry, I'm just so shocked to speak to you after all this time.'

'Yes, it has been a very long time. But somehow, it feels like yesterday. You received my letter?'

'It arrived a few days ago. It's taken me a while to pluck up the courage to phone you.' She decided not to mention the detective agency.

'I can understand that. It took me a little time to, as you say, pluck up the courage to write to you.'

'I would say 56 years was a lot more than a little time.' Nancy said, trying not to sound sarcastic.

'This is true. But I had other things happening in my life. As I said in my letter, I waited until my wife sadly passed away. It didn't seem right to contact you before.'

'How did you know where to write?'

'The Internet is an amazing thing. I searched for Nancy in Dashford-on-Sea, and you and your holiday cottages appeared at the top of the list.'

'Unlike Hans Schmidt. There are lots of those, but none of them appeared to be you.'

He didn't say anything for a moment. 'Well, we've found one another now. I'm glad you called. We have very many things to talk about.'

He was right there. No point in beating about the bush. 'Such as why you disappeared.'

'I promise I will explain that to you, but there is much to tell you first to make it make sense. And I would prefer to explain all that to you face to face.'

'You're meeting Hans where?' Olivia sounded incredulous when Nancy phoned her.

'The cafe we used to go to in the Bois de Boulogne. It's a public place. I don't see a problem.'

'You're travelling all the way to Paris just to say hello?'

'It's only a quick flight. I haven't been to Paris for years. It will be good to go there again.'

'He is luring you to a foreign country where you've got no backup. That sounds dangerous to me.'

'I'm a fully grown woman with a black belt in karate. I've been trekking in the foothills of the Himalayas, and I've swum in shark-infested waters in Australia. I don't think meeting an octogenarian in a Paris cafe is that dangerous by comparison. You wouldn't bat an eyelid if I said I was meeting him in London.'

'I would. He disappears without a word, then pops up half a century later, and there's no trace of him having ever existed. It all sounds extremely dodgy to me.'

'What do you think he's going to do? Attempt to kidnap me? I need to find out what went on all those years ago. I don't want to go to my grave not knowing.'

'As long as you don't go to your grave in the course of finding out. Why can't he come to London?'

'Neither of us suggested it. I can fly to Paris as quickly as I can get the train to London. Perhaps he's nostalgic for France?'

Olivia huffed. Nancy could picture her shaking her head in disgust. 'Who's going with you?' Olivia asked.

'No one,' Nancy said.

'No one? Are you insane? Why aren't you taking Mark?'

'He's in Italy with Lucy. I don't want him fussing around me anyway.'

'Why don't I come with you? I could do with some excitement.'

Nancy considered the suggestion. The trip would be more fun with Olivia around, but she still wanted to meet Hans alone.

'OK then, but on one condition: you will not interfere.'

'As if I would. Well, actually, I would if he looked dodgy.'

'Olivia!'

'Alright, I promise not to interfere. When are we flying out?'

'Tomorrow morning.'

'Tomorrow?? But I've got a hairdresser's appointment.'

'Don't worry. I'll go on my own.'

'No, no. I can reschedule Julian. I'm sure he won't charge me when I explain that I'm saving my best friend from potentially becoming a people trafficking victim.'

Nancy laughed. 'At least you'll have something interesting to talk about when he asks about your holidays. I'll meet you at Orly airport at 12.30 pm.'

33

Mark walked into the hotel room and casually threw his camera on the bed. 'How did it go?' he asked.

'Perfectly!' Lucy smiled as she closed the lid on her laptop. 'The laptop connected straightaway. I can hear everyone clearly now that Kizzy has setup that new meeting microphone gadget for the conference room. Even the video held up.'

She got up from the dressing table where she'd been working and hugged him. Harry had confirmed that everything went well at the Birmingham end too, so there was no reason why Lucy couldn't keep her side of their marketing business going while she and Mark went travelling.

'Did you enjoy your afternoon?' she asked.

'I did, but I'd rather you'd been there,' he said, putting his arms around her waist.

'I need to work sometimes.'

'I know.' He started kissing her neck.

'Come on them. What did you get up to?'

'I took a lot of photos and posted a few on Instagram,' he said. 'I sat and watched the world or, to be more accurate, the tourists go by while I drank a hideously expensive coffee in St Mark's Square and enjoyed seeing the likes and comments come in. I reckon we could easily build up a good social media following on our travels.'

'Why would anyone be interested in us?'

'I'm allegedly quite attractive, and you don't exactly turn milk sour, at least when you've got your makeup on,' he grinned, dodging her playful slap and spinning her around onto the bed. 'How many people our age would love to be doing what we're doing now?' he added as he pinned her to the bed.

'What are you planning? An Only Fans channel?'

He did an excellent job of appearing to give Lucy's suggestion serious consideration. 'That could bring in some extra cash.'

'I hope you're joking, Mark Farnham.'

His face cracked into a smile. 'Of course I'm joking. I meant there must be loads of people who'd love to go travelling while working remotely. We could post tips and hints and look at getting some sponsors. What do you think? You're the marketing guru.'

It would be better than having him moaning about doing a job he hated. 'It could work, I suppose.'

'Good. That's settled then.' Mark flopped back onto the pillow. 'I've already planned our first Instagram-able outing for tomorrow morning.'

'What are we doing?'

'I've booked a gondola ride.'

'That sounds very romantic.' She snuggled up to him and gave him a passionate kiss.

'And I found a lovely restaurant by one of the smaller canals. It has excellent reviews but isn't extravagantly priced, so I've booked us a table for 7.30 tonight.'

'But that's three hours away. Any thoughts on what we should do to kill time before then?' she asked, undoing the buttons on his shirt.

'I hadn't, but I'm getting the impression that you have.'

'I thought we could get in some extra practice in case we need that Only Fans account,' she said, undoing his belt.

Mark didn't look too disappointed at her suggestion.

The following morning, Lucy was snuggled up in Mark's arms as their gondola floated towards the Bridge of Sighs. 'This is the life,' she said.

'Come here, you,' he said, turning to kiss her as they passed under the bridge. 'That's it now. You're stuck with me forever.'

'What do you mean by that?' Was he making some sort of proposal?

'It's what the legend says. If you kiss someone under the Bridge of Sighs, you will always be together in eternal love. I suppose we should get married now.'

What had he just suggested? 'You suppose we should get married?'

'Yeah. I want to marry you. What do you think?'

Was this another one of his wind-ups? But he did sound sincere. *Laugh it off, just in case he's not serious.*

'Only you could propose on a romantic boat trip in one of the most romantic cities in the world and make it sound like a casual invite to the cinema.'

'Everyone has to have a talent for something.' He looked her straight in the eyes. 'So what's your answer?'

He was serious then. Lucy hadn't been expecting that at all. But was it that outrageous an idea? Not really. Ever since they'd met, she'd felt he could be 'The One', and living together hadn't changed that. *Go for it, Lucy Thomson!* 'I suppose we could get married. Yes!'

'Good. That's sorted then.' He sat back in the seat, looking pleased.

'Is that it?'

'What else are you expecting me to do? I'd probably fall in the canal if I went down on one knee.'

'A kiss would be good!'

'We've just done that.'

'Seriously? Are you rationing them now?'

'I don't want to wear my lips out,' he said, pouting them for effect.

'I don't recall you being worried about that at 6 o'clock this morning.' She leaned over and kissed him again.

'I thought that was at sunset?' Em said when Lucy FaceTimed her from a café later.

'What do you mean?'

'You're only bound together in eternal love if you kiss under the Bridge of Sighs at sunset.'

Lucy grinned at Mark. 'You proposed to me under false pretences!'

'It would've been sunset somewhere in the world,' Mark said. 'I'm sure whatever god or goddess of love is looking down on us won't mind. Anyway, we couldn't do it at sunset - we won't be here this evening.'

'Ooh. Where are you off to next?' Em asked.

'Unfortunately, we're off to see the olds,' Lucy said.

'I thought you liked going to your mum and dad's?'

Lucy's parents' villa was luxuriously fitted out. She particularly enjoyed using their infinity swimming pool, with its holiday brochure-standard views across the Tuscan countryside. Her mum and dad had been living there permanently for the last two years. 'It's warmer than Moseley,' her dad had said when they announced they were moving.

Lucy sighed. 'I do usually. But Mom will love Mark.'

Em and Mark both looked confused. 'Is that a bad thing?' Mark asked.

'No, but I'm not ready to share you yet. We'll barely have any time alone. She was threatening to invite a few neighbours around tonight to show you off like a prize pig. When I tell her we're engaged, she'll go into overdrive. She'll have the entire village lined up to greet us, complete with flags and a band.'

Em laughed. 'I can picture her doing that.'

Mark looked thoughtful. 'That would look great on our new Instagram account.'

'What new Instagram account?' Em asked.

'Mark and Lucy On Tour - all one word. I set it up last night,' Mark said. 'You can follow all our adventures on there. I'm going to create a website to go with it as well.'

Lucy looked sceptical. 'As you can tell, Mark has influencer aspirations now.'

'You'll be live streaming your wedding next!' Em laughed.

Mark looked as if he were considering it.

Lucy glared at him. 'No!'

'But think of the sponsorship potential.' He had that serious look again. Hopefully, he was winding her up. Lucy decided to ignore it.

'Will you be my maid of honour?' she asked Em.

Em looked down at her bump. 'If you're getting married soon, I'm not sure Bob's bump will look good on the livestream.'

'Your bump will be fine,' Mark jumped in. 'We could do a whole piece on the do's and don'ts of choosing dresses for pregnant bridesmaids.'

'As your marketing expert,' Lucy said in her most professional voice, 'I would advise you to stick to one niche: travel blogging. Don't try to incorporate wedding content as well - you'll just confuse our audience. I'm saying that as your future wife as well.'

Mark saluted her. 'Well, future wife, I better do as you say. In which case, could we squeeze in a couple of nights in Rome after we see your folks? It would give a bit more variety on our feed.'

Lucy raised her eyebrows at Em.

'Don't complain,' Em said, 'You could be stuck at home like me. I'm so envious of everyone gadding about abroad.'

'Everyone? Who else is gadding about, then?' Lucy asked.

'Nancy and Olivia. They flew to Paris this morning.'

'Mum's in Paris?' Mark said. 'She didn't mention it.'

'They only planned it yesterday. Your mum said something about revisiting some of their old haunts.'

'I'd forgotten they lived there for a while. I suppose I better text her the good news then.'

Lucy was shocked. 'You're going to text your mother to tell her we're engaged?'

'Yes. What's wrong with that?' He looked genuinely puzzled.

'I thought such momentous news would warrant a phone call at the bare minimum.'

He shrugged. 'If you insist. But if she's busy, she'll be less annoyed by a text.'

Lucy couldn't imagine Nancy being annoyed by a phone call announcing her youngest son's impending marriage, but she'd have that discussion with Mark in a minute. 'We better go. We've got a train to catch,' she said to Em.

Mark finished his espresso and looked at his watch. 'We need to get our bags from the hotel.'

They walked across the square arm in arm. 'I could get used to this.' Lucy said.

'Good!' He smiled. 'So could I.'

Lucy's phone buzzed as they crossed the final bridge before their hotel. It was a text from her mother.

GO HOME NOW

She showed it to Mark.

'Have you upset her?' he asked.

'If I have, I don't know how. She doesn't normally send shouty texts. I better phone her.'

Lucy's mother answered immediately. 'Darling! Thank God you're alright.'

'Hello, mumsy. Of course I'm alright. What's up?'

'Oh, Lucy! I'm so afraid. They're imprisoning people in their own homes.'

What was she talking about? 'Who are?'

'The police.'

'But why would they do that?'

'It's just been on the news. There's an outbreak of this Wu-Tang Clan thing in northern Italy. They've blockaded the roads to stop people from getting out.'

Ah, the new flu virus in China. Lucy wasn't surprised it had got as far as Europe, but it hardly warranted her mother's overreaction. She wasn't normally this flakey.

'It's just a different sort of flu, Mum. I'm sure we'll all be fine.'

'Fine? Are you mad? Someone's died already. I've sent your father out to get toilet paper.'

'Why on earth are you doing that? Diarrhoea isn't a symptom.'

'It isn't, but the thought of running out of loo roll is almost as horrifying as dying. But never mind that. You two have to go home now. I couldn't bear it if you caught it. The worry would kill me.'

Lucy tried to reassure her. 'It will all blow over. It's just the media exaggerating everything.'

'It's real, Lucy. Don't come here. We'll be like one of those deserted plague villages before you know it. Please promise me you'll catch the next flight back to Birmingham, London, anywhere you can, as long as you get away from here.' She was almost in tears.

This was getting ridiculous. Lucy adopted her most confident tone, which had never failed to reassure clients who were getting cold feet about implementing a new marketing strategy. 'Don't worry, Mum. I'll check it out then I'll let you know what we're going to do. Love you.'

'Always remember that I love you too.'

Mark looked at Lucy as she ended the call. 'Did you hear any of that?' she asked.

'Bits.'

She could see he was distracted by the news feed on his phone. He read out the title of the first article in the list. 'Virus sweeps Europe.'

Lucy looked over his shoulder at the rest of the headlines. There were more variations on the same theme. Several referred to tourists being quarantined in Tenerife.

Mark looked thoughtful. 'Rome might not be such a good idea. We should wait a week or two before booking our next trip. See how this all pans out.'

Lucy felt deflated. 'You're not getting cold feet about our plans, are you?'

'No, of course not. But I don't fancy being locked up in a hotel full of ill people. Do you?'

'You know how the press goes over the top about stuff like this. It might even work in our favour - if they keep on bigging it up, people will be too scared to go abroad and we could bag some holiday bargains.'

He laughed. 'This is why I love you. You always look on the bright side.'

'Every cloud and all that,' she said, kissing him.

'But I still think we should go home.'

Lucy's phone buzzed again before she could tell him not to be so pessimistic. It was a call from Kizzy. 'I don't want to say I told you so, but I did warn you.'

'About what?' Lucy asked.

'Making big decisions. Do you want me to see what flight I can get you on?'

Lucy was annoyed. This defeatist attitude was spreading faster than Covid. 'Has my mother called you?'

'No. I thought you must have seen the news. They reckon the Foreign Office will advise against travel to Northern Italy any minute now, so I'm being my usual efficient self and getting the two of you out of Venice ASAP.'

Mark raised his eyebrows at Lucy. She knew him well enough to recognise that was his 'I told you so' look.

'Thank you,' she said to Kizzy, realising that she was outnumbered on this one. 'I guess that's the sensible thing to do.'

34

Nancy and Olivia emerged from their hotel and got into the taxi the receptionist had ordered.

'This traffic is horrendous,' Olivia said as the driver made his way slowly through the rush hour. 'It wasn't like this when we lived here.'

'That's why I allowed plenty of time. We'll arrive well before Hans, I'm sure,' Nancy said, trying to hide any trace of the nervousness she was currently feeling. She'd woken at a ridiculously early hour this morning, convinced that Hans had turned into a miserable old man who was just after her money. Olivia's negativity about the whole exercise had obviously seeped into her subconscious.

'At least the weather is good,' she added, looking up at the patches of blue sky between the fast-moving clouds.

'I'm taking a detour to get you there faster,' the driver told them in French as he turned down a narrow side street.

'I recognise this road,' Olivia said. 'Can you turn left at the corner, please,' she asked.

'That's in the wrong direction, madame,' the driver said.

'I know, but we used to live around here. I'd like to see a few familiar landmarks on the way.'

The driver shrugged and did as she asked.

'The bookshop,' Nancy said, recognising the steep steps up the front door of a shop. 'What is it now? I can't read that.'

'A tattoo parlour,' Olivia grinned. 'Inflicting pain on its customers in a slightly different way to Madame Dubois. Rue de la Dordogne next, please.'

The driver took another couple of turns until they were climbing up the familiar steep, narrow street. Nancy's shoulders started aching, remembering the heavy suitcase she'd carried up there that first day.

'They've repainted number 27,' she said as the driver pulled over to let another car pass. 'That deep blue front door looks far more welcoming than that awful sludge brown colour.'

'Shall we ask him to stop so we can see if anyone's in?'

'No, that's enough reminiscing for one day.' Nancy was impatient to get to the café just in case Hans had had a similar idea about arriving early.

Olivia raised her eyebrows. 'I thought that was the whole point of this trip.'

'In a way.'

'Anywhere else?' the driver asked.

'No, thank you,' Nancy said.

He navigated back to the main road.

Ten minutes later, Nancy and Olivia were standing on the footpath that ran past the cafe in the Bois de Boulogne where Hans used to meet Nancy after work.

Olivia took charge. 'Here's the plan: We'll watch the cafe from over there.' She pointed to a wooded area opposite the cafe. 'When we see Hans arrive, you will go up to his table. I will continue to watch what's going on from a distance. If you put your shoulder bag on your left shoulder, I'll know you need rescuing.

'But I always put my bag on my left shoulder.'

'Ok. Your right shoulder, then.'

'You're taking this far too seriously. I'm sure I won't need help.'

'He might not be the man you remember.'

Nancy laughed. 'I can guarantee he won't be the strapping 24-year-old who swept me off my feet.'

'You know what I mean. It could still be someone pretending to be him.'

Nancy sighed. 'Alright then. How will you help exactly?'

'It depends on what's happening. My instincts are usually good. I scared off that man who tried to rob the mini-market around the corner from my house a few weeks ago.'

'Woe betide any man who tries to get between you and your Petit Chablis. Anyway, Hans and I always used to go for a walk after we had a drink. He might want to do that.'

'I'll follow behind at a discrete distance.'

Nothing about Olivia was discrete normally, so this could be worth seeing or hopefully not seeing.

They were by the clump of trees now. Olivia led Nancy into the undergrowth. 'We've got a good view from here.'

Nancy looked across at the cafe. It hadn't changed much over the years. It might be painted a slightly different shade of green, but it still had tables dotted around in front of it, shaded by red and white umbrellas advertising beer. There was no sign of anyone who looked even vaguely like Hans.

Olivia looked at her watch. 'T minus 10. I can't remember, was he punctual?'

'Always,' Nancy said. Hans had only kept her waiting once: that fateful day when he disappeared. She hoped he was on time today because Olivia's edginess was becoming infectious. She was regretting accepting her offer of support.

A brown-haired man with a stick and a slight limp walked up to the cafe and dropped into a seat at the nearest table, obviously relieved to be able to sit down.

'Is that him?' Olivia asked.

'Not unless he's shrunk.'

'People do you know.'

'Not eight inches. That man is barely 5ft 6.'

'He's got a good head of hair.'

'You mean he's got a good wig maker. There is no way a man of his age has hair that thick. And how has it got darker? Hans was always a natural blonde.'

'He might be dying it now.'

A woman joined the man at the table. They could hear them speaking in fluent French.

Not Hans, then. Nancy breathed a sigh of relief.

'What about him?' Olivia nudged Nancy and looked to the left of the cafe.

Nancy saw a man walking around the corner of the cafe. White hair. Clean shaven. Tall. Something about the way he carried himself reminded her of Hans.

He sat at the table they always used to sit at if it was free. Her heart started racing. 'I think it is him,' she whispered to Olivia.

'He doesn't look too threatening. Still want to talk to him? We can walk away if you don't.'

'I've not come all this way to bottle out. Wish me luck.'

Olivia held her back. 'Look around in case there's someone poised to pounce on you.'

'What are you suggesting? That a criminal gang has forced him to sit there to lure me out into the open, like some wild animal they want to trap.'

'You mock, but it could happen.'

'Oh, for goodness sake.' Nancy removed Olivia's hand from her shoulder and strode purposefully towards the cafe.

As she got nearer to the table, Nancy took a deep breath to steady her nerves. *Calm down! You're behaving like a lovesick teenager. Hans will explain exactly what happened in 1964. You will listen, and assess how plausible his story is. You might hug and exchange a few pleasantries, then go your separate ways.* Except, despite her inner voice's advice, she didn't want him to go. *How can you possibly know that? When he starts talking, you might decide to look for an excuse to leave as soon as possible.*

The man looked up. 'Nancy?'

The years had been kind to him. Despite the paler, more wrinkled skin, he still had that same mischievous look in his blue eyes that had drawn her to him the first day they met. She slipped into the seat opposite him.

'Thank you for coming to Paris,' he said. 'It is wonderful to see you again. May I?' he asked, sliding his hand across the table and taking her hand in his.

She smiled back. He lifted her hand and gently kissed it. The touch of his lips on her fingers sent jolts through her body in places that hadn't felt that sensation for a long, long time. *Nice to know those parts of you still work.*

'It's lovely to see you too,' she said.

They gazed at one another in silence for what seemed like hours. A polite cough broke the spell.

'I'm sorry to interrupt Monsieur, Madame, but would you like a drink?'

35

'Can we go for a walk like we used to do?' Hans suggested. 'It will be easier to talk about the past walking side by side without anyone to overhear us.'

Nancy had anticipated his suggestion, but it was still frustrating. They'd only made small talk while they drank their coffees. She'd discovered he got married in 1974, had two children, a boy and a girl, and was now a grandfather to twins. He'd worked for a car manufacturer in the export office until the Wall came down, then he'd moved back to Berlin and started freelancing as a book translator until he'd officially retired 15 years ago. He had skillfully deflected any attempt she made to turn the conversation around to 1964.

Why was he being so evasive? Nancy was even more intrigued now. She glanced across at the shrubbery. No sign of Olivia. 'Yes, let's walk by the lake,' she said.

While Hans settled the bill, Nancy texted Olivia.

`Going for a stroll`

Her reply arrived just as Hans came back to the table.

`Ok will follow at a distance.`

'Do you need to answer that?' he asked.

She didn't want to admit that Olivia was planning to stalk them. 'No, it's just my son updating me on his plans.'

Hans smiled. 'Shall we go?' She got up, picked up her shoulder bag and followed him onto the path.

'This way, I think,' he said, heading to the left.

They walked in silence for a few minutes while several joggers and a dog walker overtook them. Nancy glanced over her shoulder. There was no sign of Olivia. Either she'd lost them, or she was very good at hiding.

Hans must have noticed her looking around.

'Is something bothering you?'

'No, everything's fine.'

Another text buzzed on Nancy's phone. She glanced quickly at it.

`Eyes on`

Olivia had been reading too many thrillers. Nancy glanced around again. Still no sign of her. How could she possibly see them if Nancy couldn't see her? Perhaps her eyesight was worse than she thought. Nancy made a mental note to book an optician's appointment when she got home.

'Life was a lot simpler without those,' Hans said, nodding at her phone.

'Yes. I'll put it in my pocket so we're not disturbed again. Let's talk.'

'I'm not sure where to start.' He seemed on edge.

'How about why you left without so much as a note?' Nancy said, successfully keeping her voice calm.

'That wasn't my choice. But my story will sound extremely strange unless I tell you something else first.'

'Go on then. Explain.'

'Perhaps we could sit there?' he said, indicating a bench facing the lake.

Nancy huffed. 'I don't care whether we sit or walk. I just want you to tell me what you need to. And then we can go back to our normal lives.'

He nodded. 'I'm finding this difficult.'

'I can see that.'

He sat down on the bench. Nancy reluctantly sat next to him. He held her hand. She liked the way it felt. She could be 20 again. *If it wasn't for all the wrinkles and liver spots,* her inner voice helpfully pointed out.

'I was a spy.'

Nancy laughed and pulled her hand away. Olivia had been right.

He looked surprised at Nancy's reaction. 'I'm not joking.'

'I'm laughing because Olivia suggested you and Dieter were both spies, and I dismissed it out of hand. I thought it was fantastical, but clearly, I was wrong.' So wrong. So much for thinking her judgement of people was always spot on.

'Why did Olivia think that? We were so careful.'

'We? So you were both spies?'

He looked uncomfortable.

Nancy filled the silence. 'Ingrid accidentally dropped some papers on the pavement when she was leaving work with Olivia. Papers that she shouldn't have been taking out of the building. Olivia put two and two together.'

Hans nodded. 'Yes. Dieter was a spy also.'

Nancy slid away from him, disappointed. She wasn't surprised, but she had hoped for a different explanation. She folded her arms and turned towards him so she could see his face properly. He didn't look at her. 'Who were you spying for?'

'For our country. For East Germany. We needed to find out what the West Germans were doing, so Dieter was selected because he was the type of man who appealed to Ingrid.'

'So it wasn't a coincidence. He didn't just make a pass at any German woman in Paris on the off chance they'd flash him a top secret document?'

'No. We all had specific targets.'

'And I was yours?' But that didn't make sense. Hans had moved into the flat beneath Olivia's months before Nancy had arrived in Paris.

'No. I was supposed to seduce Christa.'

'Which is why you took her out to dinner so often.'

'Yes. But she strung me along. I knew she wasn't really interested in me - just the food. My heart wasn't in it either, to be honest. And then you arrived.'

'Are you seriously telling me that the East German equivalent of MI6 decided having an insider on Madame Dubois's dungeon was more useful to them than someone who translated military secrets at NATO?'

'No, but I liked you - a lot. My handler was talking about sending me back to Berlin as I'd been unsuccessful with Christa. That's the conversation we were having when you saw us in the Louvre. I had to come up with an excuse to stay in Paris. I persuaded her that the information you had on Madame Dubois's clients could be useful so that they would allow me to spend more time with you.'

'So your insistence on seeing me every day and talking to me about how my day at the bookshop went was all so you could stay in Paris.'

'No. Everything I told you was true. I genuinely enjoyed spending time with you, I cared about you, and I loved you.' He looked across at her. 'I think I still do.'

He reached out to hold her hand again. This was so ridiculous. Imagine explaining it all to her sons, especially Nigel. He'd have her locked away in a secure unit before she knew it. She pulled her hand away again.

'The day you spotted me trapped on the balcony. It wasn't a coincidence that you were there then?'

'No. I was watching who came and went from the bookshop. Then I saw you appear on the balcony with the cat, and I wondered what on earth was going on.'

'And Ingrid and Dieter. Was their wedding a sham?'

'Yes, but he had fallen in love with her. We weren't meant to get romantically involved, but he did. When the Wall came down in 89, he searched for her. She was divorced from another man by then. She forgave Dieter, and now they live happily in Bavaria.'

'Sounds like a modern fairytale.' Nancy said, though it felt more like some far-fetched spy film. 'And the obscure Danish religion he belonged to?'

'All a lie. The priest was another agent. The house was one of our safe houses. The marriage wasn't legally binding. I didn't enjoy that at all. I know I said on the day that I wasn't feeling well, but it was because I was upset. I thought duping Ingrid was going too far. Ingrid had access to important documents. Dieter knew she brought them home if she was behind with her translations, but she always locked them away when he visited her flat. She refused to let Dieter stay overnight until they were married, so he never had a chance to view them. Once they were husband and wife and he moved in with her, he found out where she kept the key, and he photographed them when she was asleep at night. So, you see, she never deliberately betrayed West Germany.'

'She was heartbroken when you and Dieter disappeared.' Nancy took a deep breath. 'So was I.'

'I am so very sorry. They must have suspected I was going to defect. I don't know why. But I was walking to the bookshop that afternoon to meet you after work like we usually did, and I was suddenly grabbed by two men and bundled into a car. The next thing I remember was waking up in a cell in Berlin. They must have drugged me. They …. Well, let's say they made life very unpleasant for me for a while. They let me go eventually.'

He looked tearful. Nancy reached out to touch his arm. He looked her in the eyes. 'I would never have left you otherwise,' he said. 'Ever.'

'Why did they think you were going to defect?'

'Because that was my plan. I knew I couldn't be with you otherwise. But I hadn't told a soul at that stage, so I've still no idea how they knew.'

'Oh, Hans,' she said. She moved to kiss him, but he backed away. 'There's something else I need to tell you.'

Nancy stared at him. What else could there possibly be?

'My name isn't Hans. It's Klaus. Klaus Heidrich.'

'Well, it would be odd for a spy to use their own name,' Nancy said, trying to process it all. 'And it explains why the private detective couldn't find anything about you.'

'Private detective?'

'I paid someone to research you, but they couldn't find any trace of Hans Schmidt. Now I know why. You don't look like a Klaus to me,' she laughed.

'What does a Klaus look like?'

'I don't know, but can I still call you Hans?'

'I'd prefer Klaus. Hans has bad associations. Apart from with you, obviously.'

'I'll try,' she said. They smiled at one another.

'Any more revelations?' Nancy asked.

'No, that's everything. You know all my secrets now. Shall we walk back to the café? I could do with a beer after all that,' Klaus laughed.

'You can buy me a red wine while you're at it,' she said.

'It will be my pleasure. Do you forgive me?'

'I need to think about it. But being loyal to your country isn't a bad thing, I suppose.'

'That sounds promising.' He stood up and offered her his arm. She slipped her hand through the crook of his elbow and picked up her bag.

For a second, she thought he was going to bend over and kiss her, but a blood-curdling scream ruined the moment. They looked behind the bench to see where it had come from.

'Hello, Olivia,' Klaus said to the woman sprawled in the small ditch behind the bench.

'I told you those Louboutins weren't designed for spying,' Nancy said as Olivia sat outside the cafe. Her injured ankle was resting on another chair while Nancy wrapped it with a crepe bandage which the waiter had kindly given them from the cafe's first aid kit.

'You know I can't wear flat shoes after all this time in heels. My calf muscles are too short. Ooh.' She winced.

'Is that too tight?' Nancy asked.

'No, it will be fine. My foot doesn't need a blood supply.'

Nancy started loosening the bandage slightly. 'What I don't understand is why you decided to leap down the bank.'

'It was less of a leap and more of a step forward into nothingness, then my other foot slipped, and I made a rather ungainly appearance behind you.'

'Ruining a significant moment,' Nancy said pointedly.

'And ruining my Louboutins!' Olivia waved the shoe with the broken heel in front of Nancy. 'I thought Hans was going to assault you, and you must have too - you put your bag on your right shoulder.'

Nancy sighed. 'I put it on my left shoulder.'

'No, it was definitely your right.'

'It couldn't have been. I put my right hand through Hans' arm. I always walk on his left.'

'You sound like an old couple who've been together forever.'

Nancy smiled. 'I don't know about that, but we have the potential to be an old couple.'

Olivia raised an eyebrow. 'Even though he lied to you about who he was?'

'He had his reasons. I'm still trying to work out how I feel about those.'

'Well, I'm sorry if I got in the way of geriatric love. But you know I get confused between right and left.'

'Which is why you should have come up with another signal. If I hadn't been so distracted by the prospect of meeting him, I would've thought of that as soon as you suggested it. It should've been something more obvious, such as me calling out for help.'

Klaus returned from the toilet. 'Do you need help?' He sounded concerned.

'No,' said Nancy. 'I was … it doesn't matter. What does matter is how we get Olivia back to the hotel.'

'We could book an Uber?' Olivia suggested.

'Could we?' Klaus didn't sound sure. 'I was thinking I would flag down a taxi.'

Olivia looked disgusted. 'That's so 1964. An Uber will be far more efficient. We can wait here until it arrives. But they won't be able to drive through the barrier. You'll have to help me walk the 300 metres to get to the main road.'

'I have missed being bossed around by you,' he chuckled.

36

Nancy made Olivia comfortable on the bed, then passed her a glass of water and some painkillers.

'Has Hans gone back to his hotel?' Olivia asked once she'd downed the tablets.

'Klaus. We have to remember he's Klaus now.'

Olivia raised her eyebrows. 'Alright then. Has Klaus gone back to his hotel?'

'Yes. He's going to phone his daughter to confirm he's ok.'

'Was she expecting you to exact your revenge on him?'

'I don't know how much he's told her. I'm sure she's just concerned for his welfare.'

'So what's the next move? Are we going home now that you know all his little secrets?'

'I wouldn't call them little secrets! He's asked us to dinner this evening.'

'Both of us?'

'He's a gentleman. He was hardly likely to suggest you stay here on your own.'

'And do you want me to come along?'

The honest answer was no, but Nancy didn't have to say that out loud because Olivia knew her well enough to take the hint.

'I'm fine here. I can send for room service if I need anything. You go on your date with your hot octogenarian.'

'You think he looks hot then?'

'No. He was always more your type than mine. I've got to say, though, he's stood the test of time very well. He's the same age as my Peter but doesn't look it. Peter's like the last shrivelled old prune at the bottom of the tin - one that's been left out to go mouldy.'

'That's a bit harsh.' Nancy had thought that Olivia's opinion of her ex had mellowed since she'd seen him at their son's wedding at Christmas, but he must have upset her again. 'Anyway,' Olivia added, 'it's what you think that matters.'

'In that case, I'll text him to say it's just me.' Nancy grinned.

'What's Olivia doing?' Klaus asked Nancy when he collected her from the hotel foyer.

'She's resting her bruised ankle. She assures me she will be back on her feet tomorrow, but she's working her way through the liquid contents of the minibar to make absolutely sure.'

'That sounds very like Olivia. I didn't have an opportunity to ask earlier - what happened to Pierre?'

'He left her for another woman shortly after we ... after you disappeared.'

Klaus nodded. He obviously didn't want to be drawn into that topic again. 'Are you ok with walking to the restaurant? It's only ten minutes away. Or we can get a taxi? Or an Uber if you don't want anything as old-fashioned as a taxi?'

Nancy laughed. 'Walking is fine. I don't need a mobility scooter just yet.' Nancy put her arm through his. 'Which way?'

'Over here.' He led them down the main road.

Nancy's phone rang.

'Your son again?' Klaus said.

She quickly glanced at the screen. It was Mark. At least she didn't have to lie about that this time, but it was unusual for him to phone - he normally texted her.

'I'm sure he can wait until later,' she said, clicking the 'decline' button. 'Is your daughter ok?'

'Yes, she is happy that we are getting on. But she wants me to go home. She's worried about me catching this new virus.'

'That's probably what Mark wants to talk about too.'

Klaus nodded. 'We worry about our children from the day they're born, and then there comes a point where they worry about us.'

'Though we never stop worrying about them,' Nancy said thoughtfully.

'Let's take that side street,' he said, guiding her across the road. 'What did you do after I disappeared?'

'I tried to track down your company, but eventually, I gave up. I used to check the postbox twice a day to see if you'd sent me a letter. But then I had to leave Paris.'

'You went sailing? When I was in that cell, I used to imagine you at the tiller of a yacht, your hair flowing behind you as you sped across the waves.'

'I changed my mind about the yacht trip,' she said hesitantly.

'That's a shame. Did Patty make it around the world? We didn't get that sort of news at home.'

'No, she had to give up at Sydney. The boat had a major issue with its rigging. But on the positive side, the shipwright who looked at it for her turned out to be her ideal man. She still lives with him there now.'

They turned into another narrow street.

'Have we walked along here before?' Nancy asked. It was a typical old Parisian street, the sort you'd see in a tourist brochure. None of the tall, elegant buildings or the shops and cafés taking up the ground floor space rang a bell with Nancy, but something about the view in the distance was familiar.

Klaus smiled. 'I think you will remember it very well in a minute. I hope so anyway.'

They carried on for a few more metres, then he stopped and gently turned her around to face the building opposite. There was an old Art Nouveau clock on the wall between two windows. It had drawings of two stylised black cats curling around the clock face.

Nancy's heart skipped a beat as she recalled the previous time she'd seen that clock. She was surprised he'd remembered. 'Are we eating here?'

'Sadly, it is no longer a restaurant, but I thought you might like to see it again.'

'Did you pick tonight's restaurant so we would have to walk past it?'

'We might be making a little detour,' he whispered in her ear.

Nancy turned to face him and put her hand up to stroke his cheek.

Their eyes met briefly before he bent his head to kiss her. She felt his lips on hers. It could be 1964 all over again. She closed her eyes, enjoying the sensation as he held her close against his body. How long was it since she'd last felt this way? Years. Before Xander. Not since Hans had disappeared, to be honest.

'Can we pick up where we left off?' He whispered as he gently moved away.

'Do you mean you're going to wine and dine me, then panic and leave me frustrated at my door? ' Nancy whispered back.

'Absolutely not. I was referring to the last night we spent together.'

'Do you think we could manage a night as passionate as that again?' Nancy smiled at the memory. 'It was an impressive enough performance for a couple of 20-somethings. It would be nothing short of a miracle at our age.'

'I'm not sure I can be quite as energetic as I was when I was 25, but my heart is in it. I'm willing to risk giving it a try.'

37

'Do you have to go?' Klaus murmured as he lay watching Nancy getting dressed in the dim light from his hotel room's bedside lamp.

'Olivia and I are flying home in a few hours.'

'This isn't goodbye, is it? Please say it's not.'

Nancy hesitated. It should be. She'd wanted to solve the mystery of what had happened to Hans, and she'd done that today. Rekindling their old relationship would bring up even more painful memories. But it would be stupid to throw away what they'd clearly still got. She'd felt alive this evening in every way. There were parts of her that wanted her to stay.

And we know which parts those are, Nancy! You said when Xander died, you would finish your days in Dashford doing all the things you loved without a man holding you back.

This was so difficult. 'I don't think you could cope with me,' she said.

'Try me,' he smiled. 'Your son's nagging you to go home because of this virus. My daughter is doing the same to me. Why don't we keep them happy but carry on talking on the phone and then see where it goes? I have so much more to tell you. I'm guessing you haven't told me everything yet either.'

'Dirty stop out,' Olivia said as Nancy crept quietly into their room. 'What time do you call this?'

'I thought you'd be fast asleep.' Nancy was disappointed that Olivia was wide awake. She was hoping for some peace and quiet to think through what had happened tonight.

'Unfortunately for you, I'm often awake in the middle of the night. So what have you and Klaus been up to that kept you out till 3 am?'

'We had a lot of catching up to do.'

Olivia raised an eyebrow. 'I bet you did. And where did you do that?'

'Mostly in his hotel room,' Nancy smiled to herself.

Olivia became serious. 'Did you tell him everything that happened after he disappeared?'

'Not quite.'

'But surely you going to?'

'I haven't decided yet.'

'If you and he are going to have a serious relationship again, you will have to be totally honest with him.'

'Yes, I know. That's what scares me.'

Part Four

March 2020

38

Nancy walked into the kitchen at Dashford Grange to make another cup of tea. How many was that now? At least four this morning, and it was only 10 o'clock. This whole lockdown thing was bloody ridiculous, being stuck in this huge house with no one to talk to. What a way to spend your 77th year on the planet.

Don't wallow in self-pity, Nancy Smith. At least you're not Em. The poor girl was having to isolate at home. She'd been so excited at being pregnant, and now this damn virus was potentially a threat to her and the baby, as if pregnancy wasn't worrying enough.

Come on, Nancy. Yesterday wasn't too bad. After the prime minister's announcement on Monday night, Nancy had received an influx of emails from guests requesting to cancel their spring breaks or asking how lockdown might affect their summer holidays. Replying and sorting out all their refunds had kept her busy for most of Tuesday, but now that the flurry of activity was over, she was twiddling her thumbs.

The Dashford Women's Wild Swimming sessions had been suspended, Julie had phoned to say Pilates was off until further notice and, to top it all, she'd just received an email saying her hang gliding weekend next month had been cancelled. An hour's walk a day was no substitute for all that.

And then there was Klaus. They'd both been hoping he could visit her in Devon soon, but that was out of the question now. Yes, they could carry on talking on the phone like they had been doing every day since she'd come back from France, but it wasn't the same as physically being together. She felt a warm glow at the memory of that last night in Paris. *Don't think about what you're missing!* How bloody cruel life was, allowing them to find one another again, only to keep them nearly 800 miles apart.

It would be just after 11 am in Berlin. He'd apologised for being too busy for a phone call yesterday. Perhaps he was around now. She texted him.

Good Morning, darling. Have you got time for a chat? Xx

The message status changed to "delivered" almost immediately but he didn't reply. Nancy sighed. She'd been rather optimistic to expect him to be waiting by the phone.

She started tidying the kitchen. As she was removing an out-of-date bag of salad from the fridge, she heard her phone buzz. At last! She eagerly pulled it out of her pocket.

But it wasn't Klaus. Clive, the decorator, wanted to confirm that the paint colour he'd got for Rose Cottage's living room feature wall was correct. Strictly speaking, he shouldn't be working but they'd agreed as he was alone in the cottages and he could walk there from his house, it made no sense for him not to finish the refurbishment project. It wasn't as if it was putting anyone at an increased risk of catching Covid.

Nancy headed outside and knocked on the cottage door, then stood back.

The door opened, and a few seconds later Clive emerged, holding a paint pot lid in each hand.

'Left or right?' He asked.

'Do you mean your left or my left?'

'My left,' he said.

'In that case, your left.'

'The blood red one? Are you sure?'

'Absolutely. We're going for strong colours now, not the wishy-washy ones we've had for years. And blood red can be an engaging wall colour.'

He didn't look happy. 'Alright. As long as you're ok with it because it will take me a good few coats of paint to cover it up if you don't like it.'

'I am 100% sure,' Nancy said.

'I guess it will be practical if you have a serial killer come to stay,' he muttered as he went back inside.

'So that's my in-person human interaction for the day,' Nancy said to herself as she headed back to the main house.

Stop wallowing in self-pity, Nancy Smith. Draw up a lockdown plan.

Nancy finished drinking her tea, then made a fresh mug and took it into her study. She took a blank piece of paper out of the printer and put it on the desk. In the centre, she wrote PROJECTS TO COMPLETE DURING LOCKDOWN. Then she sat back and stared at it, waiting for inspiration to strike.

Nancy was still staring at the almost blank sheet of paper ten minutes later. How many things had she thought of doing over the years but dismissed them because she hadn't got time? Now she had all the time in the world nothing seemed important enough to bother with any more.

The doorbell rang.

Clive again, no doubt. Probably still fretting over that red paint. She got up and headed for the front door.

39

'Stop pacing! It's really distracting.' Lucy was sitting at her dining table, trying to work on her laptop.

Mark leaned on the kitchen counter, tapping his fingers on the work surface. 'I know why caged lions do it now.'

'Could you be less lion and more panda?'

'What? Sit around all day munching bamboo and refusing to shag you?'

'Fair point. Be less panda - just the sitting around element would be perfect. We're fresh out of bamboo shoots, anyway, and I can't get a supermarket delivery slot at all.'

'I spent most of yesterday sitting down,' Mark complained.

'If you're fidgety, why don't you go for a walk?' She could do with the flat to herself so she could finish off this report. She'd promised her client it would be in his inbox before noon, and there was still a chunk left to write.

'I've done my one hour outside today already.'

'I can't imagine anyone's going to arrest you if you set foot outside the door again. How will they know?'

'Cruella next door will know. She monitors my every move.'

'No one will take any notice of her. She's monitored the comings and goings of everyone in this building ever since

I've lived here. I guess it's cheaper than a Netflix subscription.'

'Hmm.' Mark didn't sound convinced. 'I suppose I could go and feed Colin.'

'Colin?'

'You know. The pigeon with the stumpy foot in the churchyard.'

'You're naming the pigeons now?'

'I thought I'd told you about Colin. He's got his eye on Martina, but she ignores him. It's quite sad. I've given him a good talking to, but it hasn't helped.'

Dear god. They'd only been locked down for two days, and it was supposed to go on for at least three weeks. What was he going to be like by then? 'Mark Farnham, have you listened to yourself?'

'What else is there to do? You've got your job to keep you occupied. I can't imagine our Instagram fans will want to see photos of the view from this flat. I finished setting up our website yesterday, and I've drafted a few potential blog posts ready for when we're allowed back out into the world again. But I've run out of things to do.' Mark looked deflated. 'I feel like a spare part.'

Lucy got up and put her arms around him.

'You're not a spare part,' she whispered in his ear. 'Parts of you are very useful.' She raised an eyebrow.

'We've done that today as well.'

'I don't remember a rule about one shag a day. I can't imagine Boris signing off on that particular piece of legislation.' She gave Mark her best come hither look. 'I could spare half an hour to distract you?'

Mark didn't look in the mood. He walked away and stared out of the window. 'I'm sorry I'm so fed up. When I moved in with you, I didn't expect us to be cooped up in this prison cell all day.'

'I doubt the cells in Winson Green are as well-appointed as this one.'

'No, but it still feels like a prison.'

He had a point. Lucy had chosen her flat in the centre of Birmingham's jewellery quarter because it was near her office and a convenient space to crash after nights out. She hadn't expected to be cooped up in it 24/7. Two days into lockdown and even she was fed up with it.

And it must be worse for Mark. Apart from his lack of a job, he was used to living by the sea. They'd taken long enough to get back together. She didn't want to lose him again. 'I know it's not what we planned. We were supposed to be sitting on a fancy veranda somewhere in the sun. But what's the alternative?'

'I might have a solution,' he said cautiously. 'How about we move in with Mum?'

Hmm. Living with her future mother-in-law. Lucy got on with Nancy, but sharing a house with her for several weeks, even one as big as Dashford Grange, had the potential to drive them all crazy.

Mark must have taken her silence as a no. 'Come on. There'd be more space down in Devon. And it will take longer to get bored of the scenery. If we coordinate our walks, we could even see Jack and Em in person at a distance, so we'd have other human beings to interact with, not just Mum.'

'But would your mum be happy with us being under her feet?'

'If she doesn't want us living in the big house, we could move into one of the holiday cottages in the courtyard. They're all empty now. No one is going to be holidaying there until lockdown is over. And once it is, we move out again and go back to touring the world.'

Lucy liked that suggestion. They'd still have some privacy if they were in a cottage. 'Have you asked her?'

'No, but I'm sure she'd go for it. She's not used to being all on her own. Shall I give her a call?'

Ten minutes later, Mark emerged from their bedroom. 'Are we moving to Devon then?' Lucy asked.

'I think we are.' He looked puzzled.

'What do you mean think? Surely it was a straight yes or no.'

'Mum said yes, but she didn't sound overly keen on having us there.'

'Well, she has always been fiercely independent.'

'I know. But I thought the prospect of being completely alone for the next few weeks would fill her with horror. She's so gregarious. I can't remember a time when she didn't have anyone around. Anyway, she says we can have one of the cottages so we don't get in one another's way.'

'That's exactly what we wanted, isn't it?' So why didn't he look pleased about it?

'It was a strange conversation, that's all. Something's off. When do you want to go? The sooner we can get there, the better, as far as I'm concerned.'

'In an hour? I've nearly finished this report.'

'Suits me. I'll start packing,' he said, heading back towards the bedroom.

'Don't you want to say bye-bye to Colin and Marina?' Lucy called after him

Mark turned back towards her and rolled his eyes. 'It's Martina - keep up.'

40

'Matt's cancelled the booking for the church hall,' Em said as she put down her phone.

'He's what?' Jack walked into the living room at Octopus Cottage holding Em's latest craving, a mug of hot chocolate.

'He's cancelled the church hall booking for June's exhibition.'

Em and Matt's art group had been planning their first joint exhibition. It was intended to be the culmination of a year of hard work, timed for the start of the main holiday season. Or it would've been if it hadn't been for Covid.

'But that's three months away. We'll all be out and about by then.' Jack sounded confident, but Matt's source had inside knowledge.

'His sister works for public health, and she reckons we'll be locked down until at least July.'

Jack sighed. 'That's not a particularly attractive proposition.'

'Better than dying of Covid.' Em didn't want to think about that, particularly now that she wasn't only responsible for herself but for Bob, too.

Jack looked concerned. 'We'll be alright, I'm sure.'

'You will, but what about me and Bob? We're classed as vulnerable.' Em stroked her stomach, which was growing rounder by the day. 'What appalling timing.'

'We're being careful. You're fit and healthy. What else can we do?'

'Nothing, I suppose.'

He leaned over and kissed her. 'I've got a Teams meeting, unfortunately. I'll be back in an hour.'

'Ok.' Em watched him get up and head for the hall door.

As he got there, he turned around. 'Why don't you check in on Nancy? She must be fed up being stuck at home on her own.'

'I guess.'

Em took a sip of the hot chocolate. It was the only thing that helped with her morning sickness. She picked up her phone and texted Nancy.

`Could do with a Zoom call xx`

No response. Nancy had been quiet all week, apart from a couple of texts when Em had asked how she was. Em worried about her being on her own. She'd been different somehow since she'd made that trip to Paris. She was off in her own world most of the time, which was not like Nancy at all. But Clive would tell Em if he noticed anything wrong, surely.

Em decided to head to her studio to work on the landscape painting she'd started yesterday. It might take her mind off her worries for an hour or two at least.

41

The journey from Birmingham to Devon had been straightforward so far, with only a handful of other vehicles on the motorway. Lucy had pretty much had the outer lane to herself.

'That has to be the quickest I've ever done this journey,' she said as she turned onto the coast road.

Mark smiled at her from the passenger seat. 'Ten more minutes, and we'll be pulling up in front of the Grange. I can feel the tension leaving my shoulders already.'

He stroked his hand along her thigh.

'Is the tension rising elsewhere instead?' She grinned at him, pleased he seemed back to his old, relaxed self.

'It might be. But we better get settled in first. I don't think Mother dearest would appreciate me having my wicked way with you in the entrance hall.'

'I bet there's been a lot of that in the past,' she grinned.

'Probably. Do you fancy a bit of role-play? I could be the country squire, and you could be the poor scullery maid?'

'Cheeky! If we're doing that, I'll be the lady of the manor, and you can play the poor gardener.'

'I see. We're going for a Lady Chatterley vibe, are we?'

Before Lucy could answer, the sound of sirens came from behind them.

Mark turned around and looked out of the rear window. 'It's a police car.'

Lucy glanced in the driver's mirror. Blue flashing lights filled her view. 'Who are they after?'

'Us by the look of it. You'll have to stop.'

'Shit! I shouldn't have tempted fate.' Lucy pulled over to the side of the road, her heart rate rising. She hadn't been speeding, so what the hell was this about?

The police car pulled in behind them. A middle-aged policeman got out of the passenger side and strode purposefully towards Lucy's car while his colleague stayed in the driver's seat.

He tapped on Lucy's window. 'Good afternoon, madam. Can you get out of the car, please?'

Lucy wasn't in the mood for being messed about or catching Covid now. 'Only if you keep your distance.'

'Fair enough.' The policeman took a step back and waited for her to open the door. 'Mind telling me the reason for your journey?' he asked as she got out.

'We're moving house.'

He peered into the back of the car, looking sceptical. 'You don't seem to have much with you.'

'We don't need a lot. We're moving into furnished accommodation.'

'That's convenient. And where would your furnished accommodation be?

'Dashford-on-sea.'

'Famous as one of North Devon's favourite holiday destinations. That Dashford-on-sea?'

Great. A sarcastic copper. That was all they needed. Lucy decided to play him at his own game. 'Is there another one?'

'I think not. Are you sure you're not going on holiday?'

'Quite sure. We're moving in with my fiancé's mother. She's old and frail.'

The policeman didn't look satisfied with her answer. 'Can I see your driving licence, please?'

Lucy leaned back into the car and asked Mark to pass over her handbag.

'Don't antagonise him,' he whispered as he handed it over.

'As if I would,' she whispered back.

She found her licence in her purse and held it out at arm's length for the policeman to read.

'You're from Birmingham,' he said, taking a step back. 'Lots of Covid in Birmingham. Where did you say you were going again?'

Was he trying to catch her out? 'Dashford-on-sea,' she said slowly and deliberately.

'Whereabouts exactly?'

'Dashford Grange.'

He smiled at her smugly. 'Where the holiday cottages are?'

'Yes. My fiancé's mother owns them.'

'Does she indeed. And what's her name?'

'Nancy Farnham.'

'Ah, yes. Mrs Farnham.'

Mark had got out of the car now. 'Is there a problem, officer?'

'Yes, sir. There is. I know your mother. I've booked her for speeding several times over the years. And I wouldn't describe her as frail. Far from it. She always gives the impression of being quite robust, to be frank.'

Lucy had no difficulty imagining how robust Nancy could be, especially when confronted by a pompous policeman like this one.

'Surely you're not expecting a 77-year-old woman to spend lockdown on her own?' Mark must have decided to appeal to PC 452's softer side.

'Except she's not alone, is she, sir?'

'I don't know what you mean.'

'She was very much not alone yesterday. I had to have words about that.'

'Who's with her then?' Mark didn't think Olivia had moved in, and Jack and Em were still at Octopus Cottage when he'd texted Jack this morning. Perhaps one of her WI friends had decided to join her.

'I suggest you ask her. In the meantime, you need to return to Birmingham. The only reason to travel is to get food or medicine or if you're an essential worker. And I do not believe any of those reasons apply to you two.'

The policeman walked to the middle of the road in front of Lucy's car, legs apart, arms akimbo. 'You can turn around there,' he said, pointing to the gateway to a field on the opposite side of the carriageway.

'But that's ridiculous, officer.' Mark sounded as annoyed as Lucy now.

'Those are the rules, sir. If you don't like them, write to Number 10. Now, are you going to do as I've requested, or would you prefer me to issue you with an on-the-spot fine? Either way, you aren't going to Dashford today.'

Mark and Lucy exchanged a look. Mark got back in the car, and Lucy followed suit.

'What are we going to do?' Lucy whispered, turning her head away so the policeman couldn't read her lips.

'We're going to turn around like good little citizens, and when they've lost interest, we'll find another way back to Dashford. There are plenty of side roads we could use instead of this one.'

'Is it worth it?' Lucy asked.

'Of course, it's worth it. No one's going to ban me from seeing my own mother. I could understand it if we'd coughed all over him. Considering pigeons are the only living creatures we've been within two metres of for the last few days, we're more likely to be carrying bird flu than bloody Covid.'

Lucy started the car, manoeuvred it onto the other side of the road and set off back the way they'd come. She looked in the rearview mirror. 'They're following us. I feel like a fugitive!'

Mark drummed his fingers on the edge of the car door. 'I bet they're planning to tail us right the way back to the motorway. They won't go much further because then we'll be Avon & Somerset's problem.'

Lucy carried on driving, keeping a close eye on the speedometer. A speeding fine would be the icing on the cake. 'What did he mean about your mum not being alone?'

'I bet he's referring to the decorator. She said he was still working there. I can imagine Inspector Morse was unimpressed by that.'

The police car followed them for 15 minutes before turning off towards Barnstaple.

'Thank God. They must have had a call to go somewhere else,' said Lucy, heaving a big sigh of relief.

'There's probably some other loving son who needs a bollocking for attempting to visit his elderly mother,' said Mark.

'Now what do we do?'

Mark started fiddling with the satnav. 'There are plenty of old lanes we could use to get to Dashford. I used to cycle around them when I was a kid.'

'Good idea. They won't have ANPR,' said Lucy approvingly

'ANPR?'

'Automatic number plate recognition. They might be tracking us.'

'I didn't realise you were so knowledgeable. Have you been on the run before?'

Lucy couldn't tell if he was impressed or worried. 'No, but I've watched *Hunted*. We mustn't withdraw any money from cash points, either. The fugitives always get caught out that way.'

'I'll bear that in mind next time I need to evade the long arm of the law,' he laughed. 'There's a left turn in half a mile.'

The turn led them down a road that soon became a deep-sided lane so narrow that the hedgerows on both sides brushed the car as they slowly drove along it.

'I'm glad there's not much traffic. This would be a nightmare otherwise. It's been ages since we saw a passing place,' Lucy said, wincing as another branch made a slight scraping noise against the paintwork.

'Don't worry. It's mostly tractors that use these old lanes.'

Lucy was horrified. 'Was that meant to be reassuring?'

'We'll be fine. They'll see us before we see them.'

Half an hour and only one tractor encounter later, Lucy drove into Dashford Grange's courtyard.

Nancy came out to greet them. 'Where have you been? You said you were ten minutes away, but that was almost an hour ago.'

'It's lovely to see you too, Mother Dearest.' Mark said as he got out of the car. 'We encountered a zealous policeman who seemed to know you personally.'

'I can guess who that is. He's loving having all these new laws to enforce,' Nancy said as she watched Mark unload the suitcases from the Audi.

'Don't I get a hug?' she asked.

'I thought you'd want to quarantine us?' Mark said.

'Don't be so ridiculous. You haven't got a temperature, have you?'

'No, I'm feeling fighting fit, and so is Lucy.'

'In that case, I insist you greet me properly.' She marched over to him and pulled him into an embrace, then she turned to Lucy and did the same.

'These are for Lavender Cottage,' Nancy said, pulling a pair of keys out of her cardigan pocket and handing them to Mark. 'It's the biggest one. You won't get in one another's way there if you need peace and quiet to work, Lucy. Clive's finished redecorating it. Put your things in there, then come over to the house. We've prepared dinner for you.'

'Have you ever met Clive?' Lucy asked as they carried their luggage to the cottage.

'Years ago, I think. Why?'

'I just wondered if he was your mum's type?'

'He's got to be at least 15 years younger than her,' Mark said as he opened the cottage door.

'Perhaps she fancied having a toy boy. Someone's been helping her cook this evening, by the sound of it.'

'Don't be ridiculous. She's beyond all that now. There hasn't been anybody since Dad died.'

'So you're saying you'll be beyond all that if we're still together when we're 77?'

'That's different. I very much hope that a fine specimen of a man like myself will still be up to fucking you senseless when I'm 77. Though I'm not sure how turned on I'll be by saggy tits,' he said, staring at her chest.

'You better make the most of them while they're still perky, then.'

'I'll take you up on that offer later,' he laughed, giving Lucy a kiss. 'Unfortunately, we have to be sociable first.'

Once they had unloaded everything into the living room, they headed over to the main house. Nancy had left the front door ajar.

'Mother dearest?' Mark called as he walked into the hallway with Lucy hot on his heels.

'We're in the drawing room,' Nancy shouted.

Lucy and Mark exchanged a glance. 'We!' she whispered and raised her eyebrows.

'Stop it! It'll be one of her WI friends,' Mark whispered back. He strode across the hall, with Lucy following him. She crashed into his back when he came to an abrupt halt in the drawing room doorway.

A tall man with white hair and glasses got up from the sofa and smiled at them.

Lucy raised her eyebrows. 'I don't think you're in the WI.'

42

The atmosphere was tense in Dashford Grange's dining room.

'More food, darling?' Nancy asked Mark.

'I wasn't expecting you to kill the fatted calf, Mother,' Mark said, looking at the array of unfinished dishes on the table. 'They do have food in Birmingham, you know.'

'I'm fully aware of how people eat in the Midlands. I grew up there, remember? However, as it's the first time I've seen you and Lucy since you announced your engagement, I thought I'd push the boat out. And it's a welcome for Klaus, too. I didn't get a chance to do that properly yesterday.'

Lucy noticed Nancy and Klaus exchanging a knowing look. They seemed very loved up. She suspected Nancy had given Klaus an excellent welcome yesterday, just not a culinary one. Mark must've seen the way they looked at one another, too. He seemed deeply uncomfortable.

'Are you planning to stay long, Klaus?' he asked, between mouthfuls of Steak Diane.

'A few months, hopefully. Then perhaps your mother can live with me in Germany for a while.'

'I'm looking forward to that.' Nancy looked genuinely thrilled at the prospect.

'Is Nigel aware of the latest developments here?' Mark asked.

Nancy huffed. 'I've been granted a slot in his diary on Friday. His PA told me he was fully booked for the rest of the week, so it's his problem if he's the last to find out. I'm sure he'll be thrilled to hear that Klaus has moved in. He's always saying I need someone to look after me.'

Lucy smiled at Nancy's mischievous grin. They all knew full well that Nigel would be horrified and would probably be seeking legal advice immediately. Not that Mark was reacting much better.

'What I'm baffled by is how you got out of Germany. I thought they locked down earlier than us,' Lucy asked.

'They did,' he said. 'But I managed to drive into France before they closed the borders. The ferries are still running. I told them I was returning to England to be with my partner. I wasn't showing any Covid symptoms, so they were happy with that, and I got to Dover without any problems. In fact, I got as far as Devon before anyone stopped me.'

'Our mutual friend by any chance?' Mark asked.

Klaus looked puzzled.

'He means the policeman, not the Charles Dickens book.' Nancy explained.

'Ah, yes. He was threatening to repatriate me until I told him my son worked in the German Embassy and it might cause a diplomatic incident.'

'Does your son work in the German Embassy?' Mark asked.

'Yes - in Helsinki,' he grinned.

Lucy chuckled. She could see what Nancy saw in Klaus.

He carried on with his story. 'Our mutual friend settled for escorting me here to check I wasn't lying, which was a relief. I didn't want to have to outrun him. I'm rusty at all that.'

Mark looked alarmed.

'More vegetables?' Nancy asked, pushing the serving plate towards him, presumably as a distraction technique.

'No more, please, Mother. I'm full now, thanks.'

'I'm sure you've still got room for dessert, knowing you,' she said, collecting his empty plate. 'It's your favourite.'

'Not strawberry blancmange again.'

'Of course not. I realise you're 37, not 7. It's sherry trifle. Will that do?'

'That would be fantastic. Thank you.'

'Klaus - give me a hand, will you.' Nancy shepherded him out of the dining room.

'You're going to be like the side of a house if she keeps this up,' Lucy said to Mark when they were alone in the dining room.

'Don't worry. The novelty of mothering me usually wears off after 24 hours.'

'Feeling more relaxed about Klaus now? He seems very nice.'

'I'm intrigued why he has previous experience of evading the law. But yes, he does seem ok.'

'Just ok?'

'Well, alright. She's obviously very pleased he's here.'

'You don't begrudge her some happiness in her twilight years, do you? If we're globetrotting, and Jack and Em are tied up with raising a family, she deserves to have someone of her own to spend time with.'

'But she's got her friends.'

'Not ones who have a twinkle in their eye like Klaus. And her friends are dwindling in number. She's outlived several of them already. Covid might see off a few more.'

'Now look who's being cheery. Klaus is no spring chicken.'

'He looks quite fit to me.'

Mark glared at her.

'Not in that way! I meant he looks healthy.'

'We'll see how healthy he looks after a few months of living with Mum. '

43

'This evening went well,' Nancy said as she snuggled up to Klaus in bed.

He put his arm around her. 'Are you sure? Lucy likes me, but I don't think Mark is happy that I'm here.'

'He'll come round to the idea. I should have said something when he phoned this morning. It wouldn't have been such a shock to see you standing in the drawing room if I had.'

'How much do they know about Paris?'

'What we did last month?'

'No, I meant in 1964.'

'Very little. I imagine they're not that interested, and I've no intention of telling them. Not that I'm ashamed, but some things are best left in the past.'

'You were always good at keeping secrets,' he said, kissing her forehead.

'Too good,' Nancy said quietly.

Klaus turned on his side and looked directly at her. 'You and I have no secrets now, do we?'

Apart from the enormous one that you've been trying to tell him for the past month. You'll have to explain now. She took a deep breath. 'There is one.'

He was looking at her intently now.

'When you asked about Patty's round-the-world sailing trip, and I said that I had changed my mind about going, that was true, but I didn't say why I decided not to go.' She sniffed. *Don't cry now!*

Klaus put his hand on her cheek and kissed her. 'It can't be as bad as my secret was.'

'Oh, but it is.' She sobbed onto his shoulder. 'I've been trying to tell you ever since we got back together, but it never seems to be the right time.'

'Sometimes there is no right time. Are you worried I'm going to be angry?'

'I don't think you will be. Not with me, I hope. But it might upset you.'

'If it does, it does. You can't keep it from me now. I promise I'll listen.'

'Ok, then.' She took a deep breath and closed her eyes. 'When you disappeared, I was pregnant with our child.'

She half expected him to push her way, but he held her tighter, not saying anything for a while. And then she realised he was crying too.

'When did you know?' he whispered.

'Not until two or three weeks after you'd disappeared. I'd been feeling rough, but I put it down to stress and not eating properly. It was Olivia who suggested I go to the doctor.'

'And the baby,' he said. 'What happened to our baby?'

'I wrote to my parents to say I wasn't coming home, I was staying in Paris. I didn't mention being pregnant, of course. But I wanted the baby to be born in England, so I secretly went back to London. Olivia helped with that. I gave birth there. I called her Anna. She was beautiful. She looked a lot like you.' Nancy sighed. 'Then I had to give her away. I remember the woman from the adoption society coming to take her. I cried for days. I've never seen her since, but I've thought about her every single day.'

Klaus looked stunned. 'Who knows?'

'Olivia. And Xander - I thought I ought to tell him in case she ever came looking for me. He was extremely kind about it. No one else knew. I left the bookshop before it became obvious. I let everyone think I'd cancelled the sailing trip and decided to travel the world on my own instead.'

'I'm sorry you had to go through that alone. I would've found a way to look after you - both of you - if I'd known.'

Nancy rolled over and grabbed a tissue from the box by the bed. 'I know you would. But what's done is done.' She dabbed her eyes.

'Have you tried looking for her?'

Nancy shook her head. 'What would she want with me? I didn't give her the best start in life, did I?'

Klaus looked thoughtful. 'But that wasn't your fault. I'm sure she'd understand.'

'It will be an interesting story to tell her if she turns up now. But she's not going to, is she? She'd have found me years ago if she wanted to.' Nancy felt tearful again.

Klaus kissed her. 'We've got each other.'

'Don't go disappearing on me again. Once was more than enough,' Nancy said.

'I'll try not to,' he said. 'Ich liebe dich, Nancy.'

'Ich liebe dich auch, Klaus.'

And this time, he didn't flinch.

AUTHOR'S NOTE

Dear Reader,

Thank you so much for reading *Be Less Panda*. I hope you enjoyed it. If you did, I'd really appreciate it if you could leave a review on Goodreads or Amazon - just a few words will do. It helps other rom com fans discover my books, which means I can write more of them.

SPOILER ALERT: This paragraph contains major spoilers, so please don't read on unless you've finished the book or you don't mind ruining any surprises. Here we go: As with all my characters, Hans, Dieter, Ingrid and Christa aren't based on anyone in particular. They're inspired by a mix of situations that I've researched. If you think their stories are far-fetched, sadly, they're not. During the Cold War, East Germany used attractive men like Hans and Dieter to seduce West German women who had access to secrets. They even staged a fake wedding in one case. Google "Romeo Spies" if you want to find out more. It's fascinating. Thank you to my husband for suggesting it would make a great subject for a novel.

SPOILERS OVER! I'm planning more books in the Dashford series in 2025. In the meantime, I'm working on

Love Me Till Wednesday, a rom com featuring a completely new set of characters, which I'll be releasing in November 2024.

To be the first to hear about any new stories, sign up for my Book Club. You'll find the link on my website:

https://www.suzannelissaman.com

With love and laughter,
Suzanne x